The Wardrobe Supervisor's Toolkit

The Wardrobe Supervisor's Toolkit: A Comprehensive Guide to Wardrobe is a complete resource for organizing and streamlining the wardrobe process for any live production, with tips and tricks to quickly and seamlessly dress performers for their next scene.

This book offers a foundation for anyone wishing to improve their wardrobe skills, as well as specific steps for universities and theater companies to implement into their wardrobe process. Elizabeth Polley draws on professional experiences to provide clear directions, numerous examples, practical forms and lists, and advice for keeping calm and bringing order to backstage costume changes. This toolkit includes paperwork samples, quick-change tricks, laundry solutions, dress rehearsal recommendations, items to have in a wardrobe kit, and much more.

This book is written for new and emerging Wardrobe professionals and costume shop managers, as well as students in technical theatre courses, including Costume Technology, Costume Design, Stage Management, and Production Management.

Elizabeth Polley is an Assistant Professor of Theatre at Albright College and the Wardrobe Manager for The Glimmerglass Festival's 2024 season. Recently, she worked as the Costume Shop Manager and Adjunct Professor for the Kean University Theatre Conservatory and Premiere Stages Theatre Company. Prior to this, she worked as a Visiting Assistant Professor of Costume Technology at the University of Louisiana at Lafayette. Highlights from Polley's professional wardrobe career include dressing for the concerts of Taylor Swift, Pink, Justin Bieber, Paula Abdul, and Ariana Grande. Her national tour wardrobe work includes *Kinky Boots, Dirty Dancing, Jersey Boys, Spamalot!, West Side Story, Beauty and the Beast, Cats,* and *Ragtime.*

The Focal Press Toolkit Series

Regardless of your profession, whether you're a Stage Manager or Stagehand, The Focal Press Toolkit Series has you covered. With all the insider secrets, paperwork, and day-to-day details that you could ever need for your chosen profession or specialty, these books provide you with a one-stop-shop to ensure a smooth production process.

The Costume Designer's Toolkit
The Process of Creating Effective Design
Holly Poe Durbin

The Literary Manager's Toolkit
A Practical Guide for the Theatre
Sue Healy

The Production Manager's Toolkit, 2nd edition
Successful Production Management in Theatre and Performing Arts
Cary Gillett and Jay Sheehan

The Voice Coach's Toolkit
Pamela Prather

The Dance and Opera Stage Manager's Toolkit
Protocols, Practical Considerations, and Templates
Dr. Susan Fenty Studham and Michele Kay

The Stage Manager's Toolkit, 4th edition
Templates and Communication Techniques to Guide Your Theatre Production from First Meeting to Final Performance
Laurie Kincman

The Wardrobe Supervisor's Toolkit
A Comprehensive Guide to Wardrobe
Elizabeth Polley

For more information about this series, please visit: https://www.routledge.com/The-Focal-Press-Toolkit-Series/book-series/TFPTS

The Wardrobe Supervisor's Toolkit

A Comprehensive Guide to Wardrobe

Elizabeth Polley

Edited by Patricia Hoffman

Routledge
Taylor & Francis Group

NEW YORK AND LONDON

Designed cover image: Zycara Jones assists Ebony Hicks into her costume in the dressing room at Albright College. Photo by Danielle Kline.

First published 2025
by Routledge
605 Third Avenue, New York, NY 10158

and by Routledge
4 Park Square, Milton Park, Abingdon, Oxon, OX14 4RN

Routledge is an imprint of the Taylor & Francis Group, an informa business

© 2025 Elizabeth Polley

The right of Elizabeth Polley to be identified as author of this work has been asserted in accordance with sections 77 and 78 of the Copyright, Designs and Patents Act 1988.

All rights reserved. No part of this book may be reprinted or reproduced or utilised in any form or by any electronic, mechanical, or other means, now known or hereafter invented, including photocopying and recording, or in any information storage or retrieval system, without permission in writing from the publishers.

Trademark notice: Product or corporate names may be trademarks or registered trademarks, and are used only for identification and explanation without intent to infringe.

ISBN: 978-1-032-54520-2 (hbk)
ISBN: 978-1-032-54519-6 (pbk)
ISBN: 978-1-003-42527-4 (ebk)

DOI: 10.4324/9781003425274

Typeset in Times NR MT Pro
by KnowledgeWorks Global Ltd.

Dedication

Throughout the process of writing this book, I had one person on my mind. I kept hearing her voice and remembering the lessons she taught me over the years. I would be remiss to submit this manuscript without acknowledging her for everything she taught me and how fiercely she believed in me and all the young professionals she has mentored over the years. That woman's name is Marjie Bell, and she is truly one of a kind.

I met Marjie in 2012 when I took a job at The Phoenix Theatre Company in Phoenix, AZ, as the Assistant Costume Shop Manager. The position was open because Marjie was retiring, and her assistant was being promoted to the role of Costume Shop Manager. I met Marjie during my first week on the job when she came in to work as a costume overhire stitcher for a show, which involved a lot of quick-rigging. Marjie was fast and reliable, and she did not suffer fools. She would joke with everyone and tease you if you weren't doing something the fastest or most efficient way. She was direct and opinionated, and you always knew where you stood with her. Once I learned to not take her criticisms personally or get defensive, I realized how much there was to learn from her and how generous she was in her teaching.

You would never have known Marjie was retired. She worked constantly, but now she could do more freelance and overhire work. She began coordinating local wardrobe crew call lists for the national tours, concerts, and events that came through Phoenix and Glendale. I was lucky enough to get on the list quickly. Sometimes we would do overhire stitching, but more often we would work as dressers. Once you were one of "Marjie's girls" (there ended up being boys too), there was a certain expectation about your skills. Marjie's people were punctual, dependable, highly skilled, conscientious, excellent problem solvers, and quick learners. Marjie's goal was for the wardrobe supervisor on any given project to say, "these are the best locals that we have ever worked with", and we got that compliment more often than not. If we didn't get it, we spent time discussing what we could have done better and if anything had gone wrong. I recall a particular show when the wardrobe supervisor asked Marjie, "who are your two strongest people" and I was one that she identified. My stomach turned in knots and my cheeks flushed. I felt the pressure to do the best job I had ever done. It turned out they said that because we were going to execute a quick-change with two performers in rapid succession in the wings closest to the stage and we had to clear out immediately because side lights were going to turn on and if we were still standing there, it would project our shadow across the stage and ruin the scene. I'm happy to say that we did this flawlessly every time, even though we had no rehearsal prior to the first performance. I can still remember the rush of adrenaline I had during that moment and the pressure I felt to make Marjie proud, which I hope that I did.

Taking pride in your work is something that Marjie modeled for all of us. She pushed us to be our best and perform at our best every single time. She also encouraged us to do it with a smile on our faces. I got to be a part of Marjie's team of wardrobe people for six years. We did countless shows together. I remember all of them fondly, particularly the few that Marjie and I worked on just the two of us. Her one-on-one mentorship is the foundation of this book and of my wardrobe career. Marjie spent 30+ years as a professional wardrobe person, stitcher, and costume shop manager and mentored countless costume designers, technicians, and wardrobe professionals, and our industry owes her an extreme debt of gratitude.

I called Marjie shortly before submitting my final manuscript. She is actually retired now and has moved from Phoenix to a place with seasons and less dreadful heat. She is of course staying busy, and I would expect nothing less from her. During our call, I let her know about the book and how thankful I am for everything she taught me and for all of the opportunities she had provided. I asked her what she would want the next generation of wardrobe professionals to know. True to form, her first thought was "Never say Oh Sh*t in the middle of a quick-change". This is a good golden rule for wardrobe, because the second a performer hears that, you lose them and they start to panic too, which isn't helpful for anyone. Then she said, "Have fun, enjoy yourself, and bloom where you're planted". I can't think of better advice, and this is something I have tried to spend my career doing. She went on to say "Don't have an ego and be cheerful. Have fun and do a good job too". I can't think of better advice, so I will leave it at that.

Marjie, thank you for everything you taught me and for believing in me from the start. Most of the information I offer in this book I learned from you. Experience is the best teacher, and you afforded me the career of a lifetime for the six years we spent together. I will be forever grateful for all the lessons you shared, the fun we had, and the caliber of work that we did. I don't have the words to express my gratitude, but I hope this book is a fitting tribute to you and I hope that I have made you proud. Thank you, Ma Bell.

Contents

List of Contributors	ix
Acknowledgments and Thanks	xi

Introduction		1
The Importance of Wardrobe		1
Chapter 1	**The Wardrobe Supervisor**	5
	Job Duties	5
	Important Character Traits and Skills	6
	Organization	7
	Unique Challenges	9
Chapter 2	**Pre-Production**	11
	Communication with the Production Team	11
	Analyzing the Script	13
	Planning and Organization	14
	Quick-Rigging Tools, Tips, and Techniques	16
Chapter 3	**Paperwork**	29
	The Power of Paperwork	29
	Actor Piece Lists	30
	Check-In Sheets	31
	Crew Run Sheets	33
	Preset Lists	37
	Laundry Charts	39
Chapter 4	**Being a Team Leader**	45
	Running Your Crew	45
	Working with Performers	47
	Creating an Inclusive Backstage Atmosphere	50
	Collaborating with Stage Management	54
Chapter 5	**Tools and Safety**	59
	Safety and the Parameters of the Job	59
	Lights	61
	Wardrobe Apron: What's in It?	65
	What (and What Not) to Wear	67
	In Case of Emergency	70
	How to Set Up Backstage Changing Areas	71

Chapter 6	Tech Week	79
	What Is "Tech"?	79
	Hours and Expectations	80
	Attending a Run-Through	82
	Costume Load-In	84
	Dress Rehearsals	86
	Quick-Changes	87
	Wig and Makeup Changes	90
	Dressing Room Organization	95
	Problem-Solving	97
Chapter 7	Performances and Costume Maintenance	99
	Refining Your Routine	99
	Consistency of the Integrity of the Design	100
	Maintaining the Costumes	101
	Daily Wig Maintenance	108
Chapter 8	Next Steps	113
	Strike	113
	Rental Returns	117
	Costume Stock Organization	118
	Creating a Record	122
Chapter 9	Teaching Wardrobe	125
	Teaching Philosophy	125
	Practical Experience	127
	Putting It All Together	129
Chapter 10	Working in Wardrobe	133
	Internships and Apprenticeships	133
	How to Find a Job	135
	Unions	136
	Nonunion Work	137
	Touring	138
	Networking	138
	Wardrobe as a Career	139

Resources	141
Author Biography	145
Glossary	147
Bibliography	151
Index	153

List of Contributors

John Anker Bow is a NYC-based performer and arts educator with over 20 years of experience. John was interviewed for and contributed to Chapter 4 (Working with Performers).

Alec E. Ferrell is an AEA Stage Manager based in Philadelphia, Pennsylvania. Alec reviewed and contributed to Chapter 4 (Collaborating with Stage Management).

Lucinda Koenig is the Wardrobe Supervisor at The Phoenix Theatre Company in Arizona. Lucinda shared many paperwork examples that are included in the book along with many of her answers to interview questions and knowledge she has shared with me throughout the years.

John Pankratz, Ph.D., is a Professor of History at Albright College in Pennsylvania. Dr. Pankratz took wonderful backstage photos at Albright College for use in this book.

Kelly Yurko, B.F.A., is an Associate Professor of Makeup at the University of Cincinnati, College Conservatory of Music. Kelly was interviewed for and contributed to Chapter 6 (Wig and Makeup Changes) and Chapter 7 (Daily Wig Maintenance) and shared the Hair Styling Product Recommendations in the Resources section.

Acknowledgments and Thanks

The Phoenix Theatre Company
   Vincent VanVleet, *Executive Director*
   Michael Barnard, *Producing Artistic Director*
   Karla Frederick, *Director of Production*

Moira Caswell, *Research Assistant*

Adriana Carolina Diaz, M.F.A., *Instructional Services Coordinator of Fine and Performing Arts at Mesa Community College*

Matt Fotis, Ph.D., *Associate Professor of Theatre, Department Chair, Director of Undergraduate Research at Albright College*

Karen Lee Hart, M.F.A., *Professor of Theatre at Kean University*

Jeffrey Lentz, M.M., *Senior Artist in Residence (Theatre/Music) and Chair of Computer Science at Albright College*

Julia Matthews, Ph.D., *Professor of Theatre at Albright College*

Patrick M. McKenna, Esq., *Gawthrop Greenwood PC*

Trent Pcenicni, M.F.A., *Assistant Professor of Practice, Costume Design at Western Carolina University*

Jen Rock, M.F.A., *Assistant Professor of Theatre at Albright College*

Jennifer Saxton-Rodriguez, M.F.A., *Associate Professor of Theatre/Film at The University of Texas-Rio Grande Valley*

Sidney Shannon, *Co-Owner of The Costume Source*

... and a huge thank you to the two people I couldn't have done any of this without, my AMAZING Mom and Dad, Patricia Hoffman and Lyle Polley. Patricia created the outline for the book from my ramblings and continued to proofread and edit every chapter as I was writing. This book would not exist without her work, and I owe my success to them both for their constant love and support.

Introduction

THE IMPORTANCE OF WARDROBE

What was the last live performance you attended? A Broadway show, opera, concert, or play? What do you remember about it? Chances are that one of the elements that stood out to you was the costumes (particularly if you are reading this book). Were there costume changes? Were they fast? Did all the costumes look fresh, clean, and crisp? Were they worn correctly? We tend to notice when something is wrong with the costumes in a live performance. A costume piece falls off onstage, a closure is not fully fastened, a performer looks unintentionally disheveled after a quick-change, something rips, or a performer's entrance is delayed due to a costume change issue. But how often do we take note when things are right with the costumes? Quick-changes are seamless, costumes are worn correctly, are in good repair, and are neat and tidy.

All of this and more is the work of the wardrobe team, and it is one of the most important jobs in a live production. It is also one of the most underappreciated and suffers from a lack of training. When you attend a live production, you may not even think about the wardrobe team working backstage. Maybe you do, but a lot of the audience probably does not. When I started working on this book and would discuss it with others, many people had no idea what wardrobe is or what the wardrobe crew does. As a Costume Shop Manager for most of my career, I get the usual questions. "Do you design all of the costumes", "Where do you buy everything", and the most common comment, "That must be so fun!". However, when it comes to running wardrobe, I have found that there is an even greater lack of awareness and understanding of what the job is, how challenging it can be, and how much training it takes to be successful.

Creating costumes for a live performance is only a portion of the job. Ensuring that those costumes are laundered, pressed or steamed, repaired,

Figure 0.1 Elyse Martin (student wardrobe crew member) performs a quick-change at Albright College.
Photograph taken by John Pankratz, Ph.D.

and prepared for the show each day is an extremely important part of the process and is the job of the wardrobe team. Although it is not always the case, where there are costumes, there should be wardrobe professionals. The wardrobe team ensures that the integrity of the costume design and the Costume Designer's vision remain intact throughout the run of a show, whether it be a single weekend, a few months, a couple of years, or decades.

It has been my experience that good training in wardrobe can be challenging to come by. Throughout my schooling, there was not a single class that covered wardrobe skills. You generally learn wardrobe by doing. Students may run wardrobe as part of a class in school gaining practical production experience, as seen in Figure 0.1, but who trains them is often a tough question. Sometimes it is an older student who has run wardrobe before, sometimes it is a professor or staff person with wardrobe experience, and other times they are left to figure it out on their own. Trial-by-fire is often the name of the game with wardrobe work, and I'm setting out to change that.

I have been lucky enough to work wardrobe on numerous live productions and with many extraordinarily talented and generous wardrobe professionals over the years. Although I am not the authority and recognize that there is always more to learn and that every person, venue, and show will require a slightly different approach, I hope to provide a foundation for those interested in trying wardrobe work. All of the tools provided in this book are meant to help build this foundation but are by no means set in stone. If something works for you, that's great. If something doesn't work for you, don't use it. If you find something that works better, do it. As with anything else, the more tools you have in your wardrobe toolbox, the more successful you will likely be.

If you are hoping to pursue a career in wardrobe or gain some experience to see if you like it, this is a great place to start. Try to find as many different wardrobe opportunities as you can, because each experience will teach you something new. Find a way to keep track of tips and tricks you pick up along the way for yourself, so that you can build your own toolkit as you progress in your career. If someone has great paperwork, don't be afraid to ask if they would share a template with you. If a show has great organization systems, take notes or pictures if you are allowed so that you can refer to it later. There is a lot to be gained from working with as many different people as you can. Sometimes you will learn what not to do, and that can be a valuable lesson also.

The thing to keep in mind when working as a wardrobe person is that every time the performer walks onstage, you are responsible for how they look from head to toe. What the audience sees when they look at them comes down to how good you are at your job. This can sometimes seem overwhelming, but with the right tools, good training, and practice, you will be proud of the job you do and understand just how important it is to get it right every single time. And when you get it right, it will be one of the greatest accomplishments you will ever know.

CHAPTER 1

The Wardrobe Supervisor

JOB DUTIES

In her groundbreaking book, *The Magic Garment*, Rebecca Cunningham states that "The wardrobe crew is the staff responsible for the orderly maintenance and use of the costumes during the run of the show ... the designer and the wardrobe crew organize the backstage changing areas and work out the logistics with the stage manager and properties crew ... once the show opens, the wardrobe crew is responsible for the repair, cleaning, and pressing of the costumes". This is a great summary of what the wardrobe personnel are responsible for during the production process. Keeping this in mind, let's take a look at some specifics of what these roles entail:

Wardrobe Supervisor	Wardrobe Crew
1. Leads wardrobe crew members 2. Creates wardrobe paperwork 3. Attends production meetings and "designer run" 4. Establishes backstage changing areas 5. Collaborates with Costume Shop personnel 6. Facilitates dry cleaning 7. Oversees maintenance and repairs of costumes	1. Checks costumes in and out 2. Prepares costumes for performances 3. Presets items backstage for quick-changes 4. Assists with dressing performers, including quick-changes 5. Performs daily costume maintenance including laundry 6. Assists with costume repairs

As with many of the jobs in the live performance industry, wardrobe duties can vary greatly depending on the venue you are working for and your specific role and contract details. These lists are meant to serve as a guide for the duties most commonly performed by the wardrobe supervisor and wardrobe crew. It is important to remain flexible and learn to adjust to differing expectations from the various companies you may work for throughout your career. The best way to think of it is that once dress rehearsals begin, the costumes are the responsibility of the wardrobe team. They are tasked with getting the costumes onto the actors at the right time and ensuring that the costumes are worn correctly (as envisioned by the Costume Designer). They are then tasked with the maintenance and repair of the costumes throughout the run of the show. This includes preserving the designer's vision after the designer has moved on to their next project. Developing the variety of skills necessary to carry out these responsibilities is the job of any aspiring wardrobe professional.

Let's discuss terminology for a minute. You may have heard the term dresser used instead of wardrobe crew member. This has been a widely used term in the industry for many years, but I prefer to use the term wardrobe crew member. If you are looking for wardrobe job opportunities, you can also look for the word dresser in the job title or description. I do not mandate the use of one term or another, I simply have my own preference.

IMPORTANT CHARACTER TRAITS AND SKILLS

So, what is the magic formula of character traits and skills that make a successful wardrobe person? **Organization** is definitely at the top of the list. With the monumental numbers of costume pieces, actors, and changes to keep track of, being organized is an essential skill for wardrobe work. It is also important to have a calm demeanor and the ability to stay cool under pressure. The nature of live performance carries with it the necessity to react quickly, calmly, and efficiently in strenuous and ever-changing circumstances. If a quick-change goes awry or a costume piece malfunctions, a good wardrobe person will think on their feet to come up with the best solution to get the performer onstage quickly and safely. While talking about working with performers, it is paramount that wardrobe people be friendly and easy to get along with. They work so closely with performers that having good working relationships is necessary for success. This doesn't mean that you can't have a bad day or be in a mood from time to time, but finding a way to keep things professionally courteous so that the overall backstage energy stays positive is an important skill to master.

Basic sewing skills are a fundamental part of the wardrobe professional's toolkit. Although it isn't always the case, wardrobe people are often the ones maintaining the costumes. The longer a particular show runs, the higher the chances are of something ripping, breaking, tearing, or otherwise needing repair. Knowing how to perform efficient mending that keeps the overall design of the garment intact while also preventing further damage is particularly useful.

Useful craft skills to learn include shoe painting, repairing, and resoling including the application of dance rubber to shoe soles. Also, a familiarity with basic millinery (hat making) so that hats and headpieces can be repaired, feathers can be maintained, and headwear can be reshaped as needed are smart skills to acquire. Jewelry creation and repair can come in handy when these sometimes-fragile accessories inevitably break. Familiarizing yourself with a variety of rigging techniques for quick-changes including zippers, magnets, snaps, and Velcro™ is invaluable.

Last, developing a working knowledge of hair and wig styling techniques and basic stage makeup applications is extremely useful. Unfortunately, not all companies hire wig and makeup professionals, but most productions do make use of hair and makeup. Performers have varying skills and experience in these areas, so being able to assist them with achieving a particular hairstyle or makeup look is helpful. Knowing how to properly apply and pin on a wig is often a necessary skill for a wardrobe person.

Don't worry if you don't have all of these skills right now or if this list seems overwhelming. Some things you will have to "learn on the fly", but if you have the opportunity to learn any of these skills from a professional, I urge you to find a way to make that happen. The more tools you have in your toolkit, the better prepared you will be for the surprises that come up as you navigate your career in wardrobe.

ORGANIZATION

What does it mean to be organized as a wardrobe professional? A large part of projecting a calm demeanor and helping the cast to feel confident in your abilities involves being organized. This includes creating and updating detailed paperwork for tracking costume pieces, quick-changes, tasks during pre-show, run of the show, post-show (often called your "track"), laundry schedules, and more. Organization also requires storing and moving all the costume pieces in a consistent manner so that they are easy to locate and everyone knows where to find things throughout the run of the show. Rolling racks, hanging organizers, laundry baskets, small bins, and wall-mounted hooks are some items that help with this organization.

Developing a system to keep the costume pieces organized throughout the show, both daily and weekly, is essential to a wardrobe supervisor's success. You will want to consider the venue(s) of the performances and the set-up of the dressing rooms and backstage areas when deciding how to organize everything. Touring shows that have to load in and out quickly and frequently tend to use gondolas with hanging organizers that are self-contained and can roll onto the truck as-is. Universities and regional theaters often have dressing rooms with wall-mounted racks or rolling racks (see Figure 1.1), but hanging organizers and shelves above the racks can be useful for accessories. A variety of hanger-based organizers for each actor (often called ditty bags) are available for purchase or can easily be constructed from woven fabrics and used for many years. Ditty bags can also refer to zippered mesh laundry bags

Figure 1.1 Costumes organized in a dressing room at Albright College. Photograph by the author.

(also called lingerie bags), which should be issued to each actor for small, delicate items such as pantyhose, tights, dance trunks, and bras.

Having a comprehensive list of presets for quick-changes divided by act and side of the stage will also help you to expedite your pre-show and intermission tasks. How you format this list will depend on the show, venue, cast, and crew sizes. If you have many dressing rooms, you could divide the list per room so that you know what items to get from each room and avoid multiple trips and interrupting actors during their pre-show routine. By organizing your list by side of the stage, you can ensure that you have all items that are preset on stage left at the top of the show before going to do the actual presets to avoid running back and forth or extra trips. The more you can streamline your process, the more time you will have to deal with the inevitable last-minute issues that come up and the less hectic and stressful your show calls will be.

UNIQUE CHALLENGES

Do you have a favorite hairdresser? If so, you know the incredible feeling of sitting in their chair and knowing that you are going to look fabulous by the end of your appointment. I think that working in Wardrobe is like that in some ways and also like being a personal assistant in others. Although this can vary wildly depending on the production and your track, the relationships wardrobe people develop with performers are very personal and require a lot of trust. The performer trusts the wardrobe person to make them look great and get them onstage on time and the wardrobe person trusts the actor to follow the steps of the quick-changes to avoid mistakes or injuries. If you are working as a personal dresser, having the performer's water bottle, towel, favorite lozenge, or other items on hand during their quick-changes will help them feel taken care of during the show. This helps them deliver the best performance possible.

> **KEY CONCEPT: WHAT IS A TRACK?**
>
> A track consists of the tasks that a wardrobe crew member performs from start to finish for a single performance including all pre-show responsibilities, presets, quick-changes, tracking of costumes, post-show duties, and more. Each member of the wardrobe crew will have an individualized track for the show.
>
> Live performance can induce a somewhat chaotic, frenzied, and stressful environment backstage, particularly on large shows with many moving parts, cast members, and details to perfect. Keeping your cool backstage during a live performance is uniquely challenging and comes with practice. Remembering that panic never solves anything is an effective way to approach unexpected events backstage. Understanding the chain of command and who to go to if you need help solving a problem is an important part of wardrobe work. Thinking on your feet and coming up with a workable solution, even if it is only temporary, is going to help make the performance a success.
>
> It is important to remember that different people approach things in diverse ways, so remaining flexible and adaptable will be paramount to your success. If you are working as a wardrobe supervisor, the paperwork and information that you receive from the costume designer will vary from project to project. Learning to communicate what you need to succeed in your work is essential. Also, if you are not given information or it is given in a format different from what you are used to, try to find a way to work with it to create the paperwork you need to organize your production. Ultimately, the organization of the costumes becomes your responsibility starting at the first dress rehearsal, but you are not responsible for how it was organized up to that point. Devising various strategies for this part of the process will be an important part of your toolkit.

CHAPTER 2

Pre-Production

COMMUNICATION WITH THE PRODUCTION TEAM

As the Wardrobe Supervisor, you will want to establish an open line of communication with all members of the production team. Important relationships include the Costume Designer, Costume Shop Manager, Stage Manager, Wig and Makeup Designer, and Production Manager. You will collaborate with even more members of the team, so being included in all communications from the start of the process is important. Often the Wardrobe Supervisor will not attend weekly production meetings until very close to the start of tech, but being included in the distribution of minutes from the meetings is a great way to be in the loop and keep ahead of potential problems. Coordinate with the costume shop personnel to establish deadlines for paperwork so that you know what to expect and how to plan your workload. If possible, ask to see fitting photos and "walk the racks" in the costume shop to begin familiarizing yourself with the costume pieces. The more questions you can ask prior to the start of tech, the smoother your process will be.

The stage management team are key collaborators for the wardrobe team. They will have a good idea of entrances and exits and quick-changes as soon as staging gets underway. If your stage managers are open to creating an Entrance/Exit chart for you prior to the designer run/crew watch, it will streamline the process of timing changes and creating preliminary wardrobe paperwork immensely. I was first given a chart like this at the Phoenix Theatre Company by their fabulous Stage Management team and I have used it as a template moving forward. I request a chart like this (see Figure 2.1) on every show that I work on, particularly those with high cast counts and numerous costume changes. How to use this chart at the run-through will be discussed in Chapter 6, but requesting it from the Stage Management team as early as possible is highly recommended.

ENTRANCE/EXIT PLOT Version 1   *As You Like It*   EHP 11/08/23

Actor/Character	Pg	Line	NT Loc	XT Loc	NT Time	XT Time	Time to Change	Notes
ACT I								
Scene 1								
Actor 1/Orlando	2	1	SL		0:00			
Actor 2/Adam	2	1	SL		0:00			
Actor 3/Oliver	2	25	SR		1:36			
Actor 1/Orlando	3	77		SL		4:14		
Actor 2/Adam	3	83		SL		4:38		
Actor 4/Charles the	3	87	SR		4:43			
Actor 4/Charles the	4	160		SR		7:40		
Actor 3/Oliver	4	170		SL		7:43		
Scene 2								
Actor 5/Celia	4	1	SR		7:45			
Actor 6/Rosalind	4	1	SR		7:45			
Actor 7/Touchstone	5	27	SL		9:05			
Actor 8/Le Beau	6	89	SL		10:41			
Actor 9/Attendant	6	115	SL		11:06			Roll out the carpet for the wrestling
Actor 10/Attendant	6	115	SL		11:06			Roll out the carpet for the wrestling
Actor 11/Duke Frederick	6	140	SL		12:17			
Actor 12/Lord	6	140	SL		12:17			
Actor 4/Charles the	6	143	SL		12:23			
Actor 13/Spectator	6	143	SL		12:23			
Actor 14/Spectator	6	143	SL		12:23			
Actor 15/Spectator	6	143	SL		12:23			
Actor 1/Orlando	6	145	SL		12:34			
Actor 14/Spectator	8	215		SL		16:20		
Actor 4/Charles the	8	215		SL		16:20		
Actor 8/Le Beau	8	215		SL		16:20		
Actor 11/Duke Frederick	8	225		SL		16:53		
Actor 12/Lord	8	225		SL		16:53		
Actor 13/Spectator	8	225		SL		16:53		
Actor 15/Spectator	8	225		SL		16:53		
Actor 7/Touchstone	8	225		SL		16:53		
Actor 5/Celia	8	248		SR		18:00		
Actor 6/Rosalind	8	248		SR		18:00		
Actor 5/Celia	8	253	SR		18:20			
Actor 6/Rosalind	8	253	SR		18:20			
Actor 5/Celia	8	258		SR		18:40		
Actor 6/Rosalind	8	258		SR		18:40		
Actor 8/Le Beau	9	260	SL		18:50			
Actor 8/Le Beau	9	285		SL		19:57		
Actor 1/Orlando	9	290		SL		20:11		

Figure 2.1 An entrance/exit chart for *As You Like It* at Albright College.

Additional paperwork that the Wardrobe Supervisor should request comes from the Costume Designer and their team. You will want to request actor pieces lists (dressing lists) and come to an agreement on a deadline for those to be finalized, with the understanding that things will continue to shift throughout the tech process. These lists are essential for your wardrobe paperwork and for successfully executing the Costume Designer's vision. Examples of these lists and how to use them will be discussed in Chapter 3.

The Wardrobe Supervisor is the advocate for their crew and the performers whom they will be dressing throughout the show. Communicating the specific needs of the wardrobe team to the rest of the production team is a very important responsibility. What will you need backstage to successfully run the show? Will you need a quick-change booth, folding chairs, laundry baskets, full-length mirrors, clip lights, hooks, pipe and drape, or other items? You should present these needs as soon as you are aware of them so that they can be considered in the backstage planning process. With scenic elements, props, performers, and other moving parts backstage, you don't want to surprise people with the footprint needed to execute quick-changes. Sometimes it is not possible to have any permanent spaces backstage for changing due to a lack of space, so quick-changes need to be planned with laundry baskets and drop cloths that can be struck after each change. Is there a cross-over for crew/performers or is it a mile around the theater to get from one side to the other? Knowing the parameters of the backstage area of the theater will be paramount in your wardrobe planning.

Do not forget to communicate with the sound engineer if wireless microphones are going to be used for the production. This can affect your work more than people realize, so collaborating with the sound department is key. If wireless microphones are going to be used, check in with the costume shop staff to find out who provides mic packs and belts and when they are available. Also, is there something that can be used in fittings to simulate the size and shape of the transmitter? What is the procedure going to be for sound check and how will it affect the performers getting into their costumes for dress rehearsals? Are transmitters going to be worn in wigs? If so, will the performers need help from the wardrobe crew to secure them? Confirm who from the sound department will be backstage during performances and where they will be located, in case there is an issue with a microphone that needs to be addressed during a quick-change or when an actor is offstage. Collaborating with sound regarding wireless microphones is an extremely important part of wardrobe work. Also discussing mic placement and planning with the costume and wig staff will help troubleshoot potential issues before they arise.

ANALYZING THE SCRIPT

Whether you are signing on for a specific contract with a theater, or you have a permanent position with a company, you should always read the script as soon as possible. This will give you important information such as how many performers are involved and a rough idea of how many costume changes could be necessary. Although many of these details can be somewhat flexible and will be determined later, having a general idea of the scope of a show and any red flags to consider is a great first step.

The first read of a script (particularly one that you have not read before) is meant to understand the story, meet the characters, and get an overall picture of the show. If you are reading a musical, I highly recommend cueing up the cast recording and listening to the songs to begin to familiarize yourself with them and understand the tone/tempo of the music. Your second reading of the script can begin to focus on costume details. Is there a passage of time that could necessitate costume changes? What season are we in? What is the time period? How many performers might there be? Is there anything concerning for wardrobe in the script or stage directions? (This could include blood, food, items in pockets, undressing or dressing onstage, extreme blocking, getting wet, fighting, dancing, crawling on the ground, etc.) Making notes of any questions that come up as you read the script will help you prepare to meet with production personnel. This is also a good time to start figuring out how many wardrobe crew members the show will require so that you can discuss this with production management. Having a working knowledge of the script (and score if applicable) will be a wonderful tool as you move forward with the production. If you know when something is happening onstage, it is easier to anticipate what comes next and be prepared backstage.

If a script is not available to you in advance, or the production you are working on does not have a script, or if you are not contracted with enough prep time to read the script, your first encounter with the piece may take place at the designer run/crew watch. This can be intimidating, but it is a great opportunity to practice thinking on your feet and adapting quickly. In this case, I definitely recommend requesting an entrance/exit chart from stage management so that you can more easily track the performers throughout the show, particularly if it is not following a script. If an entrance/exit chart is not available, make as many notes as you can about when and where performers enter and exit so that you can attempt to create paperwork prior to the first dress rehearsal. Another option is to request to record the designer run/crew watch for yourself, particularly sequences where you anticipate quick-changes to occur. This would allow you to watch and re-watch the footage to decipher the timings and locations of entrances and exits. There are strict rules about copyright and recording, but sometimes this is possible.

PLANNING AND ORGANIZATION

> If You Fail to Plan, You Are Planning to Fail
>
> Benjamin Franklin

Although we understand that live performance is ever-changing and things are in flux during the tech process specifically, that does not mean that we should not attempt to formulate a plan. It is always easier to have something to start with, even if you end up with many revisions before opening night. Planning and organizing as much as you can for the wardrobe process prior to load-in and the start of tech will save you some headaches during a time that is always stressful.

Where do you start with what can seem like a daunting process? First, know that you should start this process as far in advance as possible. For example, my upcoming contract as the Wardrobe Manager for The Glimmerglass Festival begins a month before the first dress rehearsal for the shows. This may seem like a lot of prep time, but there are many tasks that need to be completed to get ready. It allows time for me to go over the scores, investigate costume paperwork, check in with the costume department, create first drafts of wardrobe paperwork, attend run-throughs, organize and prepare the wardrobe room, dressing rooms, and maintenance area, inventory supplies and order necessary items, meet with and train the wardrobe staff, collaborate with the hair and makeup department, and more.

As dress rehearsals near, check in with stage management about dressing room assignments and start making lists of what goes in each room. Look at the preliminary costume plot and create a chart of when the costume changes occur. Are there multiple changes at the same time? Go through the script and determine how many lines/pages there are for each change. Make a list of the quickest changes and discuss with the costume personnel what the costume pieces are and what underdressing might be possible. Take an inventory of all of the wardrobe supplies at the theater and create a list of items that need to be ordered. The first time you go to do laundry is not a good time to find out the detergent has run out. Do you need more items for backstage? (These can include laundry baskets, racks, clip lights, mirrors, hanging organizers, folding chairs, and more).

Figure 2.2 Hanging accessory organizers backstage at The Phoenix Theatre Company. Photograph taken by Matthew Bates.

Figure 2.3 Wardrobe Crew Members Hannah Martin and Isabella Boehm consult and update paperwork during a dress rehearsal at Albright College.
Photograph taken by John Pankratz, Ph.D.

Organize all of the paperwork you are receiving and creating in one place. This can be a digital space or an actual binder, depending on your preference, but having all of your paperwork in one place will be very helpful as you start to amass all of the documents for the show. If you are doing it digitally, be sure to share access to those files with all of the people who could possibly need it (costume personnel, production management, stage management, and crew members). If something terrible were to happen to you during a production, you want other people to have access to the information needed to successfully run the show. Keeping your paperwork organized and accessible is an important tool for success as a Wardrobe Supervisor. If you create a template that you love for your wardrobe paperwork, keep a blank copy of it in your digital files that you can then copy and utilize as a starting point for each production. Some productions will require more or different paperwork than others, but having a general outline to start with will save you time moving forward.

QUICK-RIGGING TOOLS, TIPS, AND TECHNIQUES

During the costume construction process, you may be consulted by the costume technicians regarding your preferences and the needs for quick rigging of specific costume pieces. In some instances, you may not be working with costume staff, or you may be remounting a production that was done before but discover that some things have changed and the costumes require additional quick rigging. Familiarizing yourself with quick-rigging tools and techniques is very beneficial to you as a wardrobe professional, whether or not you are the one facilitating it. Quick rigging refers to changing the closure of a costume piece or accessory to make it easier and faster to put on or take off of the actor. The most common methods for quick rigging are hook and loop tape (usually referred to as Velcro™), snaps, snap tape, elastic, and magnets (see Figure 2.4). Zippers can also be considered a method of quick rigging, depending on their application. There are pros and cons to each method, and as a wardrobe supervisor, you will develop your own preferences depending on the situation. Things to consider when determining if quick rigging is necessary and if it is, which method to use, are the amount of time for the change, if the garment needs to be quick to get into or quick to get out of or both, if the change takes place onstage or offstage, if the change will be assisted by a wardrobe crew member or performed independently by the actor, the practicality and function of each option, and the total number of pieces and parts involved in the change. Let's discuss the options, their pros and cons, their functionality, and how best to utilize them.

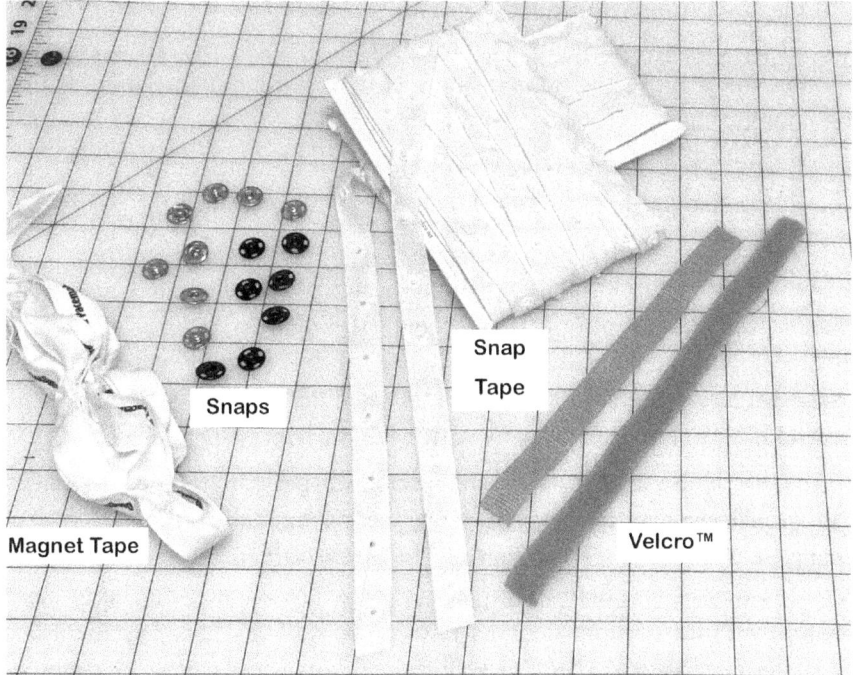

Figure 2.4 Quick rigging supplies pictured left to right: Magnet tape, snaps, snap tape, and Velcro™.

Photo taken by the author.

Velcro™ is great because it is fast for putting on and taking off. The problem with Velcro™ is that it can be loud, particularly for taking off. If you are working in a small theater space on a quieter show, the noise of Velcro™ may not be desirable. Another problem with Velcro™ is that it can mar or damage the costume piece itself, depending on the fabric, or other costume pieces it comes in contact with, particularly in the wash. Velcro™ is not a good choice for delicate fabrics. Velcro™ is best suited for button-down style closures. It should not be used for an on-stage change, unless the ripping sound is desired and the visual of Velcro™ is not problematic. If you choose to use Velcro™ for fastening a garment, follow these steps:

1. Remove the buttons from the garment.
2. Cut 1"–1.5" long strips of ¾"–1" wide Velcro™ tape, both the hook (rough) side and loop (soft) side.
3. Use scissors to slightly round the corners of the Velcro™.
4. Attach the loop (soft) side of the Velcro™ strips to the right side of the shirt placket, centering the strips over the spot where the buttons had been sewn, with the strips running vertically along the placket. Use a sewing machine to stitch around the strips, as close to the edge as possible.
5. Lineup the garment top over bottom to determine the placement for the hook (rough) side of the Velcro™ pieces, placing them over top of where the buttons had been sewn (on the wrong side of the placket). Sew these on in the same fashion as step 4, using a thread color that closely matches the shirt. Trim all your threads.
6. Reattach buttons, centered on top of the buttonholes on the right (top) side of the garment, so that it will look buttoned when the Velcro™ is fastened.

Remember to check with the costume designer or costume staff about how the shirt will be worn prior to quick-rigging it. Will it be buttoned all the way up? In Figure 2.5, you will see that the top two buttons were left functional, because they were not going to be closed when the costume was being worn. You do not want to quick-rig any buttons that will not be closed.

Velcro™ is also a great option for accessories, particularly those that need to look like they are tied in a bow, but there is not time during the quick-change to tie or untie them. It can also be used to attach a pre-tied necktie to a button-down shirt. Before performing any of these quick-rigging options, confirm with the costume designer or costume staff that it is permissible, as these steps will **PERMANENTLY** alter the costume and cannot be restored. Please note that you will need to try the accessory on the performer to mark the desired size before completing this type of quick rigging. Figure 2.6 shows a bow tie that was quick-rigged with Velcro™ at the center back.

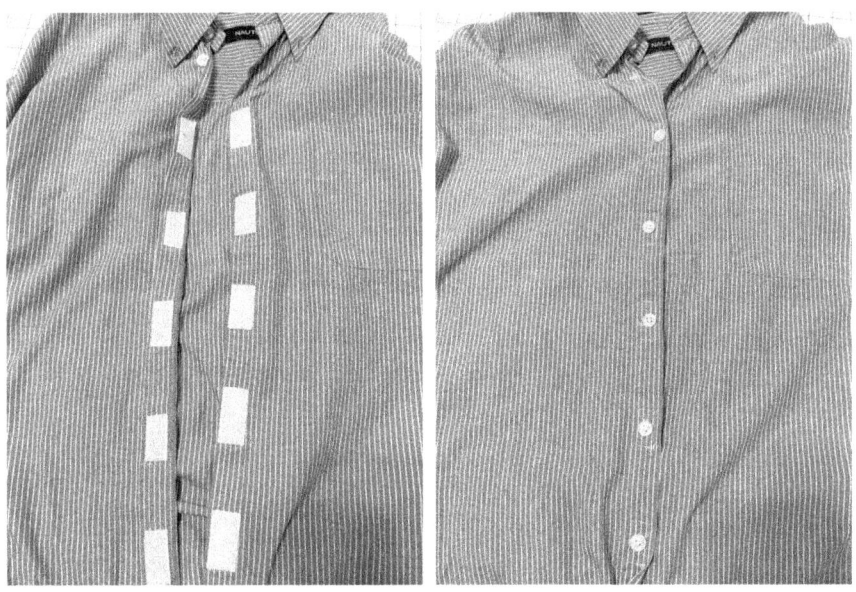

Figure 2.5 Button-down shirt quick-rigged with Velcro™. Shirt open on the left and closed on the right.
Photograph taken by the author.

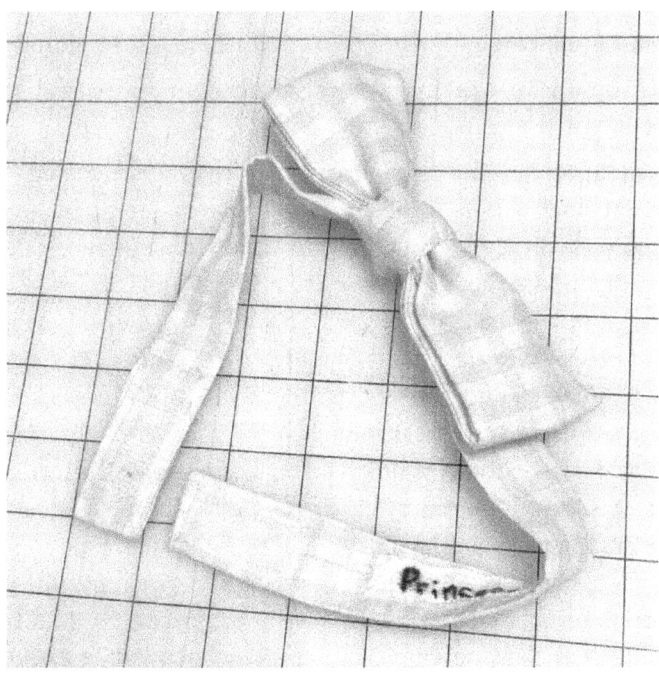

Figure 2.6 Bow tie with a Velcro™ quick-rigged closure at center back.
Photograph taken by the author.

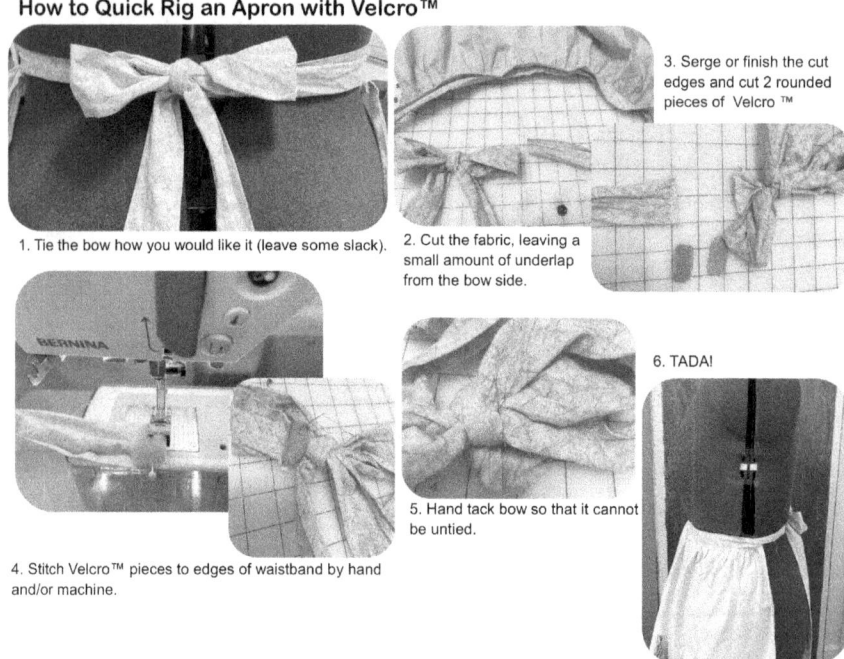

Figure 2.7 Step-by-step instructions on how to quick-rig an apron with pictures and the finished example displayed on a dress form.

Photographs and instructions courtesy of the author.

To quick-rig something that needs to look tied, refer to Figure 2.7.

To quick-rig a necktie that will be worn with a button-down shirt, refer to Figure 2.8.

Snaps are another great option for quick rigging. Snaps do not make loud noise, so that can be a big benefit. They also come in a variety of sizes and colors, so they are adaptable as far as functionality. Snap tape is a great product where small plastic or metal snaps are attached to a tape or ribbon that can easily be machine sewn down either side with a zipper foot attachment. This saves the time of hand sewing both sides of each individual snap, which can be time-consuming. Snap tape is great for rip-away costume pieces because you can unfasten some of the snaps prior to the rip-away moment, especially if it will take place onstage. This will allow the costume to easily be removed by either the performer or other performers onstage. If at all possible, I recommend dyeing the snap tape to match the garment, because it is only available in white and black and the white can show through on many colors and fabrics. Snaps can be used to replace buttons if the garment only needs to come off quickly, because they are not particularly fast to fasten. They can also be used if an actor will be buttoning or unbuttoning a costume onstage, because they can be easier to

How to Quick Rig a Necktie to Attach to a Shirt

  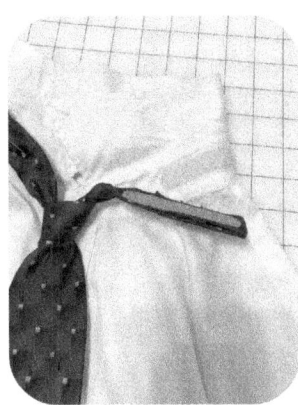

1. Knot the tie how the Costume Designer prefers and make sure it is the appropriate length.
2. Cut tie, leaving 4" on each side ABOVE the knot. Stitch hook (rough) side of Velcro™ to the side of the tie that goes to the overlap side of the shirt.
3. Stitch loop (soft) side of Velcro™ to collar stand of button-down shirt in the corresponding position.

4. Attach the non-Velcro™ side of the tie to the collar stand on the opposite side of the shirt via safety pin, tag gun, hand basting, or machine basting. Remove for washing.

Figure 2.8 Step-by-step instructions on how to quick-rig a necktie and button-down shirt with pictures.

Photographs and instructions courtesy of the author.

work and line up than buttons and buttonholes. To quick rig a button-down garment with snaps, do the following (see Figure 2.9):

1. Remove the buttons from the garment.
2. Choose the snap size and color you want to use, and make sure you have a set for each button.
3. Hand-sew the positive side of the snap to the wrong (bottom) side of the garment, centered underneath each buttonhole, using thread that matches the garment*.
4. Hand-sew the negative side of the snap to the right (top) side of the garment, centered on top of where the button was sewn, using thread that matches the garment.
5. Make sure snaps line up and function correctly.
6. Reattach buttons, centered on top of the buttonholes on the right (top) side of the garment, so that it will look buttoned when the snaps are fastened.

*Some people prefer to alternate positive and negative snaps on both sides to reduce the risk of snapping the wrong ones together. You may experiment with this technique to see if it is your preference. I have found that putting the positive side on top creates the most secure bond.

Elastic is another excellent quick-rigging tool. Two of the most common uses I have seen are for shoelaces and shirt cuffs that button. For shoelaces,

Figure 2.9 A button-down shirt quick-rigged with snaps, shown open on the left and closed on the right.
Photograph taken by the author.

thin, round elastic that most closely resembles shoelaces is best and can usually be purchased in white and black. For colors, you need to dye the elastic or paint it with fabric markers. Using plastic, heat-shrink tipping on the ends will help make it easy to lace up the shoes. If you cannot find round elastic, eighth-inch or quarter-inch wide flat elastic can also be used. Replace the shoelaces with elastic and have the performer try them on and tie them as usual. You may need to shorten the ends of the elastic, because it is stretchy, so they will require less length than the original shoelaces did. Hopefully the actor will now be able to slip the shoes on and off, which will save the time of tying or untying them during a quick-change.

For shirt cuffs, quarter-inch wide flat elastic is a lifesaver. A small chain stitch done by hand along the outer stitching line holds the cuff "closed" when wearing, but the elastic allows the actor to shove their hands through quickly in a fast change (see Figure 2.10). Another option here is elastic cufflinks if the shirt has French cuffs (see Figure 2.11).

Last, magnets are a wonderful quick-rigging tool. They are fast for both going into a garment and coming out of it and do not make loud noise. They are now available on tape as well as individual units. If you use individual magnets, such as the rare-earth magnets, which are my personal favorite because of their strong bond, you will want to sew small pouches of fabric that closely match the costume piece to house the magnets. You can then stitch the pouch with the magnet inside by hand or machine to the garment.

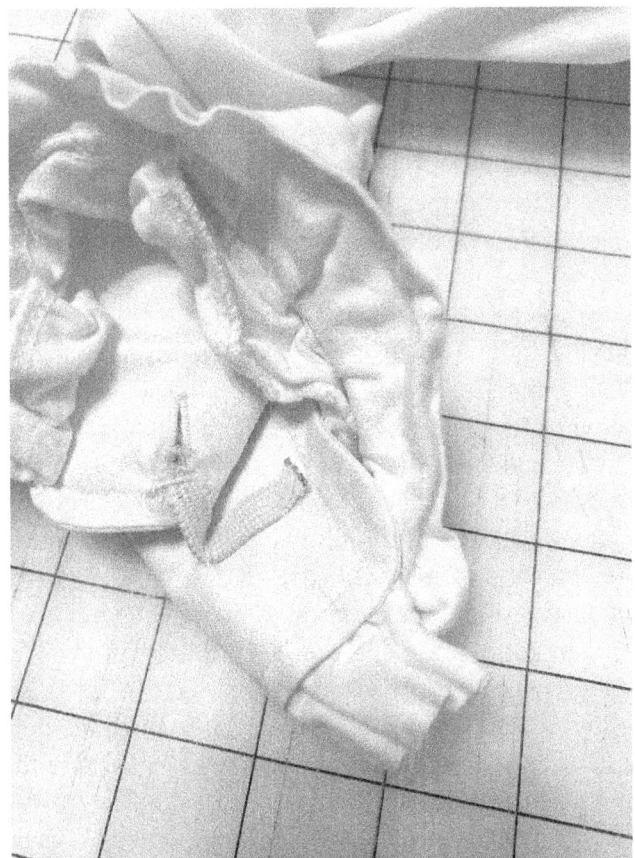

Figure 2.10 The inside of a shirt cuff quick-rigged with elastic.
Photograph taken by the author.

Magnet tape can be sewn by machine, although you will have trouble with it sticking to the throat plate of your sewing machine. This brings me to the negative side of using magnets, they can stick to things that you don't want them to. If your quick-change setup includes metal folding chairs, that can be a problem. Anything metal in your wardrobe apron or jewelry

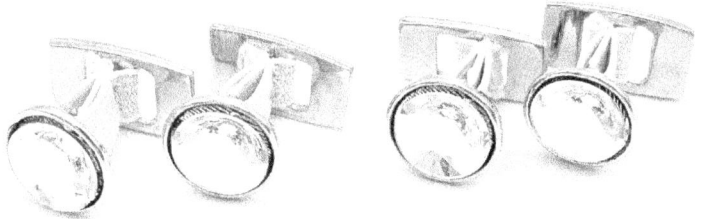

Figure 2.11 Elasticized rhinestone cufflinks available from The Costume Source.
Photograph taken by David Kaley.

the performer is wearing or anything else backstage or onstage that is metal can be a problem. I have even heard from sound professionals that some magnets can cause problems with microphones or other sound equipment. If you are going to use magnets, be sure to discuss it with everyone on the production team to be sure it is not going to cause problems. Also, you will need to be diligent if the costume is pre-set, so that the magnets don't stick to each other before you want them to, or to anything else. I have used magnets successfully, and I will share two of my favorite examples. For a musical, one of the performers was flying via harness. They needed to wear a hat while flying and then take off the hat onstage when they landed. The hat continued coming on and off throughout the show, often onstage. It was also the type of hat that perches on the head, at a jaunty angle, with a period-styled wig underneath. The wig designer and I collaborated to attach two magnets in both the hat and the wig, so that the performer could easily perch the hat on their head at the desired angle and it remained secure for flying, choreography, and staging, but the hat could easily be removed or put back on onstage and it looked great every time. In another instance, a performer had to don a vest quickly onstage, and it had to be fastened for the rest of the scene. No other performers could help with this, and the performer was struggling to fasten the vest quickly enough. The director and costume designer preferred that it not be Velcro™, because the vest was also taken off onstage and they did not want the noise. We swapped out the closures for single magnets, following the same steps as snaps, but creating fabric pouches for each magnet out of a scrap of the garment fabric, and it worked perfectly. The performer, director, and costume designer were thrilled with this solution. Another favorite use for magnets is to quick-rig jewelry. Traditional necklace or bracelet closures can be swapped out for magnetic closures to make them extremely fast to close (see Figure 2.12).

Figure 2.12 Magnet tape, individual sew-in magnets, and magnetic jewelry clasps, all available from The Costume Source.

Photographs taken by David Kaley.

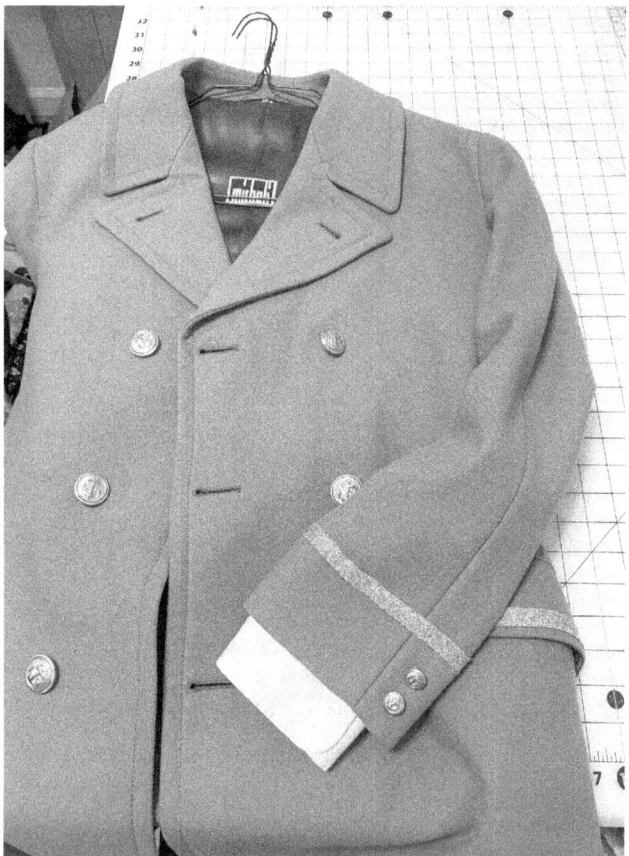

Figure 2.13 Overcoat with shirt cuffs attached to the bottom of the sleeves. Costume designed by Jennifer Saxton-Rodriguez.

Photograph taken by the author.

Specialty quick-rigging comes in many forms and refers to any combination of the techniques described here or other techniques utilized to make a costume faster to put on or take off. Some examples of this include building costume parts into other pieces so that there are fewer pieces total to deal with Figure 2.13. depicts shirt cuffs that are sewn into an overcoat, so it appears that the performer is wearing a shirt and a coat. The performer always wore a scarf with the coat, so a shirt collar was not necessary, just the cuffs. This saved time in quick-changes and allowed the performer to be more comfortable by only wearing a T-shirt underneath this warm overcoat.

You may need to get creative when it comes to quick rigging. For a musical that I worked on, the chorus all had football pants. To complete the look, they had belts threaded through the belt loops of the pants that were made of grosgrain ribbon, which was not stretchy. There was a scene where the pants needed to be put on onstage quickly, and the belt needed to be fastened. With some troubleshooting, the solution was to cut the ribbon into segments so

Figure 2.14 Football pants quick-rigged with individual segments of ribbon and a snap closure. Costume designed by Samuel Garcia.
Photograph taken by the author.

that it looked threaded on the outside, but it was not continuous on the inside, which allowed the pants to stretch. We were able to machine stitch the ribbon segments at the edges with a zigzag machine stitch. We then attached a snap to the belts at center front, which was much quicker for the performers to fasten onstage but created a strong hold to withstand choreography. We also laced the front of the pants with elastic instead of the original laces. The elastic could be tied in advance, so the performers did not have to deal with it onstage (see Figure 2.14).

Another great specialty quick-rigging option is stitching hair into hats. If they need to be put on or taken off quickly, this can save on time and help things look the way the designer intended. You can either attach weft, which is a bundle of hair extensions sewn onto a fabric strip, or part of a wig, or an entire wig, depending on what the look is. For a production I worked on, the design was very whimsical, so we utilized braided yarn to create pigtail braids and sewed them into a bonnet, which looked great and saved time for the performer during their many quick-changes in and out of this costume (see Figure 2.15). You will also notice a hair comb sewn in at the center front to keep the bonnet from slipping backwards when worn due to the weight of the braids.

These are just a few of the many specialty quick-rigging techniques that can be utilized. Familiarizing yourself with quick-rigging options, tools, and techniques can help you troubleshoot quick-changes and other issues with costume pieces. Being able to speak competently about your quick-rigging preferences and why something will or will not work will help you

Figure 2.15 Straw bonnet with yarn pigtail braids sewn in. Costume designed by Jennifer Saxton-Rodriguez.
Photograph taken by the author.

communicate with the costume technicians you work with. If you are in a situation where you need to alter garments to incorporate quick-rigging yourself, knowing these techniques and basic hand and machine sewing skills will be a great help. Thinking creatively and collaborating with others about what will work best to solve a particularly challenging problem can lead to amazing solutions.

CHAPTER 3

Paperwork

THE POWER OF PAPERWORK

As with most things, the better organized you are as a wardrobe supervisor, the more successful you will be. One of the keys to good organization is good paperwork. I have seen more formats, versions, and styles of paperwork than I would ever have imagined, and I'm sure there are plenty that I have yet to see and would be impressed by. The key is to use a format that works for you and your team and be open to the possibility of changing it whenever needed. Different shows, different crews, and endless other scenarios may all necessitate different types of paperwork. The more paperwork versatility you have in your toolbox, the better.

When all else fails, write it down and fix it later. Even quick, handwritten notes on the back of another piece of paper are better than nothing. We tend to believe we have amazing memories and will remember all of the minor details later when we sit down to update our paperwork. I have learned over the years that I simply cannot rely on my memory when I am faced with an onslaught of details, changes, and updates. Making notes of things and updating your paperwork as soon as possible improves your chance of getting those details right for the next time.

Another consideration when creating your paperwork is that we may not always be there. Personally, I refer to this as the "in case I get hit by a bus" strategy (which causes many of my crew members to roll their eyes after hearing it 100 times). As much as we don't want to think about it, illness, injury, and other personal emergencies are a reality that need to be considered when creating paperwork. Drafting notes, run sheets, and other paperwork that only makes sense to the person who wrote it is largely unhelpful if someone needs to run that track in an emergency. Worse than that is not writing things down at all and running your track from memory and being the one who does everything for everyone but doesn't keep a record of what those tasks are. I've heard this referred to as a hero track. Many amazing

DOI: 10.4324/9781003425274-4

people are guilty of this, they like to put on their "superhero cape" and save the day. It is also a method that I see inexperienced managers use to run things. Sometimes they make the mistake of assuming they can only be important if they know things that no one else knows and use it as a form of job security. I made this mistake as a young manager and thankfully learned the error of my ways. If you keep things to yourself or run things from memory and then miss a performance for any reason, it will be extremely difficult for anyone to run your track successfully, which in turn hurts everyone on the team and the production itself. Delegation and information sharing are imperative to the success of a wardrobe supervisor. Now that we know why paperwork is important, let's take a look at the paperwork I find most useful when working on a production and some samples of different formats.

ACTOR PIECE LISTS

Actor piece lists are often created by the Costume Designer in coordination with the Costume Shop Staff. As a wardrobe supervisor, make sure that you have access to any digital platform used by those creating these lists and that you are receiving any real-time updates being made to them. I recommend having a conversation with the Costume Designer or Costume Shop Supervisor to set a deadline for the Piece Lists so that you can use it to work on all the paperwork you need to create for the production. Understand that the Piece Lists may change throughout the process, including dress rehearsals, but having something to start with is extremely beneficial.

Once the Piece Lists have been created, I like to format them so that I have one for each actor in the production. This should list the scene, page number, or song when they wear each costume and each item they will wear, including accessories. The list should go in chronological order through the show, working from their first costume and ending with their final look. Listing items in the order the actor should put them on can also be helpful. If you have any additional information about how something is styled (for example, sleeves rolled up or shirt untucked), including that on the Piece List for the actor can be helpful (see Figure 3.1). I spoke with Lucinda Koenig, who is the Wardrobe Supervisor at The Phoenix Theatre Company about paperwork, and she said, "I have also begun to put much more info on the performer's individual costume plot/piece list. I list their entrances/exits and how much time they are offstage as well as the location of the change. This helps when communicating with the performer and discussing their changes … it also helps the swing/understudy to have a written record of where they need to be".

Posting the actor piece lists at the performer's individual stations in the dressing rooms can be helpful for them to follow along and see what to wear when. If performers do not have individual stations, giving them each a copy of their piece list to keep with them is also good.

As You Like It   Actor Pieces Lists   Updated by EHP 9/28/2023

Actor #6
Show: *As You Like It*
Character: Rosalind

Scene/Page	Character/Look	Item
(All Show)	Base	Tan Tights
A1S2 / p. 4	Rosalind / Look 1	blue and white striped dress
		Tan oxford heels
		Blue and white fabric belt
		dusty pink hat
A1S2 / p. 8	Rosalind / Wrestling Match	Gold chain with pendant (given to Orlando)
A1S3 / p. 9	Rosalind / Look 1	Repeat Look 1
A2S4 / p. 15	Rosalind as Ganymede / Look 2	Olive green overalls
		Tan thermal
		Grey flat cap
		Tan socks
		Brown ankle boots
		Dark brown jacket
A3S2 / p. 23	Rosalind as Ganymede / Look 2	(reading a paper)
	INTERMISSION	
A3S4 / p. 31	Rosalind as Ganymede / Look 2	Remove jacket
A3S5 / p. 32	Rosalind as Ganymede / Look 2	Remove cap
A4S1 / p. 36	Rosalind as Ganymede / Look 2	Push up thermal sleeves
A4S2 / p. 40	Rosalind as Ganymede / Look 2	Repeat 4.1
A5S2 / p. 45	Rosalind as Ganymede / Look 2	Repeat 4.1
A5S4 / p. 48	Rosalind as Ganymede / Look 2	Repeat 4.1
A5S4 / p, 50	Rosalind / Wedding	white lace maxi dress
		White bridal fascinator
		white full slip
		Tan oxford heels

Figure 3.1 Actor Pieces Lists created for *As You Like It* at Albright College.

CHECK-IN SHEETS

Check-In sheets can be used to check the costumes in before each show and check-out the pieces at the end of the show. It can feel time-consuming and tedious to do this, but it is much better to know if something is missing with time to look for it and figure out a solution than in the middle of the show when there is no time. This holds true for a check-out procedure, which greatly reduces the risk of leaving something behind if you are working on a touring show or a performer accidentally wearing a costume piece home and forgetting it for the next show.

  Check-In sheets can easily be created from the information listed on the Piece Lists. The only change is that you can eliminate items that are repeated,

As You Like It   Costume Check In/Out

		12-Nov IN	12-Nov OUT	13-Nov IN	13-Nov OUT	14-Nov IN	14-Nov OUT	15-Nov IN	15-Nov OUT	16-Nov IN	16-Nov OUT	17-Nov IN	17-Nov OUT	18-Nov IN	18-Nov OUT	19-Nov IN	19-Nov OUT
Actor 1 "Orlando"	work pants (navy dickies)																
	Tank Undershirt																
	Grey/blue/tan plaid button down																
	Suspenders (grey)																
	Newsboy Cap																
	Black Socks																
	Black Ankle boots																
	cream thermal bottoms																
	beige athletic shorts																
	black dance boots																
	cream thermal long sleeved shirt																
	white banded collar button down shirt																
	"sling" arm wrap																
	silver print vest																
	floral buttonaire (attached to vest)																
Actor 2 "Adam"	light blue button down work shirt																
	navy coveralls with belt																
	navy bucket hat																
	brown work boots																
	brown socks																
	white v-neck undershirt																
"Sir Oliver Martext"	black cassock																
	black dress shoes																
	black dress pant																
	black shirt with white collar inset																
	black socks																
Actor 3 "Oliver"	grey dress pants																
	gray suit jacket																
	blue dress shirt																
	tie																
	grey suspenders																
	dark blue sweater vest																
	black dress shoes																
	gray fedora																
	black socks																
	white v-neck undershirt																
	Brown Tweed Pants																
	Tweed brown suit coat																
	flower buttonaire (attached to suit coat)																
	white dress shirt																
	brown dress shoes																
	Brown tweed vest																
	yellow floral tie																

Figure 3.2 Costume Check-In/Check-Out sheet created by Danielle Kline, Wardrobe Supervisor for *As You Like It* at Albright College.

are removed, or otherwise listed more than once on the list. Your check-in sheets should list each performer and then every costume piece and accessory provided to them. To the right of that, it should have columns for a check-in and a check-out for every performance date. I like to fit as many of them on a sheet as possible to reduce the amount of them I need to print out for my crew. An additional idea is to group costume pieces that are preset outside of the dressing rooms together on a separate sheet and items in the dressing rooms on another sheet. This can make the check-in process much faster. See Figure 3.2 for a sample check-in/check-out sheet.

CREW RUN SHEETS

Run sheets are created for each member of the wardrobe crew and a master sheet that lists each crew member's individual track so that the supervisor/manager can see everything that is going on at one time. There are hundreds of ways to format run sheets, and the answer is that whatever works best for the supervisor and the crew is the method that should be used. I have been given laminated notecards with a hole punched in one corner and put on a metal ring to be worn on a lanyard around one's neck or tucked in the wardrobe apron. This method utilized one notecard for each change, and you could flip them around on the ring as you went through the show. This was a great idea for once things are set for a production, particularly if it is going to run for a long time and various wardrobe people will be running the track. Simpler versions of run sheets can be printed out on standard paper, usually in a landscape format, and often contain tables or lists.

What should be included on a run sheet? Absolutely everything that a wardrobe crew member does, from pre-show, through the show and post-show. If they do different things on given days or performance numbers, that should be indicated as well (for example, on Sundays, empty the steamers completely and run steamer cleaner through them, or every eighth performance, replace the insoles in a particular pair of shoes). Items on the run sheet should include enough details so that whoever runs the track can understand what to do, but not so much information that the paperwork is overly cumbersome. This can be a difficult balance to achieve, and talking with crew members about what works for them is especially helpful.

Let's look at a run sheet created for a musical at The Phoenix Theatre Company by their Wardrobe Supervisor, Lucinda Koenig (names and show details have been removed) (see Figure 3.3). This page is from the master run sheet and lists the pre-show tasks for the team and some of the presets for quick-changes. Note that this document is 24 pages in total, so this is a very busy show for the wardrobe team.

The next example is from a specific track for a wardrobe crew member (see Figure 3.4). Noted here are five quick-changes for Actors #4 & #5, including

Figure 3.3 The first page of a master wardrobe track created by Lucinda Koenig for The Phoenix Theatre Company.

Updated: 12/24/2018   Show Title   Wardrobe: Male Track 2 (Dresser #1)

ACTOR	Exits Removes	Adds	Enter	Time	Crew	Notes
		Song Title #1 change after song				
Actor #5	SL2 Character #3 - Trench Coat. Catch/Fold Discards; Put in Basket.	Character #4 - Uniform Shirt/Jacket/Cap Help w/Tie Velcro & Jacket Velcro.	SL2	3:30	Dresser Initials	Wait for Actor #4.
		1.6 - Scene Title #1 change before scene				
Actor #4	SR2 Character #1 - Vest/Tie/Shirt/Pants/Shoes Catch/Fold Discards; Put in Basket.	Character #2 - Pants/Tunic/Hat/Shoes Hand Off Tunic; Zip. Open Belt Velcro if needed; Make Sure Belt Isn't Twisted.	UC	2:45	Dresser Initials	Wait for Actor #5.
		Song Title #2 change before song				
Actor #5	SL1 Character #4 - Catch/Fold Discards; Put in Basket. Fold Black Pants; Set Aside w/Black Shoes to Reset. (next Hand Off Tunic; Zip. Open Belt Velcro; Make to basket/in front of chair)	Character #5 -	SR1	1:45	Dresser Initials	Repeat Black shoes & black pants 1.9
	TRACK #4's Loafers & #5's Security Cap to QCB. Return to Chairs. HANG Discards on Hangers. TRACK back to QCB. (along w/red hoodie & pants) Return by End of Song w/Hangers (2 Shirt/2 Pant) Hang on Handles.					
		Song Title #3 change before/during song				
Actor #4	SR2 Character #2 - Catch/Fold Discards (Zip Tunic & Close Belt Velcro); Place in Basket.	Character #3 - He rests before dressing himself.	SL1	5:15	Dresser Initials	
Actor #5	SR2 Character #5 - Catch/Fold Discards (Zip Tunic & Close Belt Velcro); Place in Basket.	Character #6 - Hand Off Pieces if Needed. He Dresses himself.	SL2	3:45	Dresser Initials	
	TRACK #4, #5, #10 & #13's Green Sneakers to QCB. Return to Chairs. HANG Discards on Hangers. (Hat Horsehair Loops over hook of Tunic Hanger) TRACK to QCB. Return to Chairs. RESET Black Pants on Chair (Under White Shirt; Place Pink Stripe Socks on Pants), Place Shoes in Front of Chair.					

Figure 3.4 A page from a run sheet for a specific wardrobe crewperson's track created by Lucinda Koenig for The Phoenix Theatre Company.

1.1 - Base to Character #1

Set Girl 1, Actor #1 & Boy coats at portal (Actor #1 hat on prop table)
Hand off coats & hats to **Actor #2 & Actor #3** (newspaper in pocket)
Wardrobe Crew #2 hands off to Actor #4 & Actor #5

During 1.2 - 1.3 - Track Actor #6 hat to SR, Actor #7 hat from SR

1.4

Actor #7, Actor #3 & Actor #4 hat hand-off

Actor #8   Chair 3   Character #1 coat

During 1.4 - Track Character #2 coats & hats to SL hall (keep Actor #8's hat for 1.9)

1.5

Part 1 - Base to Character #3

Actor #9   Chair 3   Character #3 apron, ascot   Wardrobe crew #2 snaps back closure

Set Actor #10 Character #4 at stairs

Part 2 - Base to Character #4

Chair 1	---	
Chair 2	**Actor #9**	Character #4 (black pants underdressed) - Wardrobe crew #3 help
Chair 3	---	
Chair 4	---	
Chair 5	**Actor #4**	Character #4 (overdress black pants)
Chair 6	**Actor #2**	Character #4 (no pants change)
Stairs	**Actor #10**	Character #4 (black pants underdressed) - Wardrobe crew #1 help

Part 3 - Base to Character #5

Hook 1	Actor #11	Character #5 (no gloves or hat)
Hook 2	Actor #12	Character #5 (no gloves or hat)
Hook 3	Actor #13	Character #5 (no gloves or hat)

1.6

Actor #2   Chair 6   Zipper tie
                                       DO NOT TOUCH HAT & VEST ON PROP TABLE

Figure 3.5   A page from a simple run sheet in a list format.

some changes that are resets. There are also tracking notes and indications of when and where to hang things up or reset them. Abbreviations are used to note locations, such as QCB for quick-change booth, SR for stage right, SL for stage left, and so on. Usage of abbreviations can greatly reduce the size of a document, which can be helpful when creating run sheets that wardrobe personnel will carry with them when running a show. Be sure to indicate somewhere what the abbreviations stand for so that everyone can make sense of what they are reading. It would also be helpful to walk new wardrobe crew members through the backstage change locations prior to them running a track to ensure they know where they need to be.

Another approach to a run sheet would be something much simpler (Figure 3.5). This is a portion of a run sheet for a wardrobe crew member. This does not contain as many details (and names of performers, character looks, and wardrobe crew members have been removed), but it is a very simple track to follow. If given this sheet, a new wardrobe crew member would need to consult a piece list or costume plot to determine which pieces were needed for each character. The preferences of your crew and the needs of your production will determine what run sheet format will work best.

PRESET LISTS

A preset list can be a part of the run sheet or a separate document. Having a preset list for each backstage area that will have presets can help simplify the process (for example, stage right, stage left, and the quick-change booth could all have separate lists). Also, it can be helpful to list all the items that need to be preset from each dressing room together on a sheet or note it on the check-in sheet so that the crew member can pull those items as they are doing check-in and they will not have to enter the dressing rooms while performers are getting ready to retrieve items for presets. You may also create separate preset lists for preshow and intermission, if you will be presetting additional items at intermission.

However you organize it, creating a preset list will help make pre-setting the quick-change areas much simpler and prevent the need for repeated trips to the dressing rooms. Figure 3.6 shows a pre-set list for a production of *As You Like It*. The left-hand column lists which dressing rooms the items are pulled from and the right-hand column lists which side of the stage the items will be pre-set on. The backstage set-up for this production included hooks on the wall for the items, and each item was hung on a separate hook. If your set-up includes chairs or other places to set items, you will want to include that information on the pre-set list (such as Chair #1, etc.). You may also want to label the chairs, hooks, or other location with tape and a marker or paper attached with clear tape to avoid confusion.

With larger productions, especially, you will want to assign which crew member is pulling which items for pre-setting from each dressing room and who is pre-setting each quick-change. Sometimes items are pre-set into baskets for easy transport to backstage changing areas and the baskets can even be used for the quick-change depending on the backstage set-up. If this is the case, it is helpful to put a piece of tape or other label on the side of each laundry basket and give it a number, so crew members can easily see which

Costume Pre-set List   *As You Like It*

FROM DRESSING ROOM B
- Cream Linen Shorts (Actor 1)
- Wrestling boots (Actor 1)
- Cream thermal (Actor 1)
- White banded collar dress shirt (Actor 1)
- Silver Wedding vest (Actor 1)
- Yellow, red & blue floral print tie (Actor 3)
- Wedding flower boutonniere (Actor 3)
- Green check vest (Actor 9)
- Arm sling (Actor 1)
- Scarf and crown (Actor 16)
- Wedding flower boutonniere (Actor 7)

FROM DRESSING ROOM A
- Lace wedding dress (Actor 6)
- Bridal fascinator (Actor 6)
- White slip (Actor 6)
- Straw flower hat (Actor 19)
- Linen apron with floral embroidery (Actor 19)
- White gloves (Actor 15)
- Cream hat (Actor 15) - bobby pins

FROM HAIR & MAKEUP ROOM
- Lipstick (Actor 6) with small hand mirror
- Extra bobby pins (Actor 5 & Actor 6)

STAGE LEFT
- Cream Linen Shorts (Actor 1)
- Wrestling boots (Actor 1)
- Cream thermal (Actor 1)
- White banded collar dress shirt (Actor 1)
- Silver Wedding vest (Actor 1)
- Yellow, red & blue floral print tie (Actor 3)
- Wedding flower boutonniere (Actor 3)
- Green check vest (Actor 9)
- Lace wedding dress (Actor 6)
- Bridal fascinator (Actor 6)
- White slip (Actor 6)
- Straw flower hat (Actor 19)
- Linen apron with floral embroidery (Actor 19)
- Lipstick (Actor 6) with small hand mirror
- Extra bobby pins (Actor 5 & Actor 6)

STAGE RIGHT
- Arm sling (Actor 1)
- Scarf and crown (Actor 16, given to Actor 13)
- White gloves (Actor 15)
- Cream hat (Actor 15) - bobby pins
- Wedding flower boutonniere (Actor 7)

Figure 3.6   The costume preset list for *As You Like It* at Albright College listed both by dressing room and backstage location.

basket contains the items needed for their specific change. This would then be noted in the run sheet (for example, wardrobe crew #1 takes basket #3 to change actor #4 from character #1 to character #2).

Making a note on the pre-set list reminding crew members to double check their pre-sets after completing their pre-show and intermission duties can be helpful in avoiding mistakes. Sometimes the crew member pre-setting something is not the crew member who will be executing the change, so having both crew members double check things is recommended. Another technique for avoiding forgotten items is to format the pre-set list as a checklist, with boxes to the left of each item. You can then place the list inside of a plastic sheet protector and crew members can cross off items with a dry erase marker as they set each item. Felt can then be used as an inexpensive eraser so that the sheet protector checklist can be reused. If you are working with crew members for the first time and it is feasible within your preshow or intermission duties, you may also double check presets for accuracy. However, I do not recommend making this a continuous practice. An important part of leadership is delegation and having your crew members be responsible for things helps them to feel ownership and magnifies their importance in the process.

LAUNDRY CHARTS

Laundry charts and schedules are an important part of the wardrobe paperwork and planning, particularly the larger the number of individual costume pieces is for the production. Depending on the company you are working for and the union membership status of the performers, there may be specific guidelines you are required to follow concerning the cleaning of costume pieces, mandated by the Actor's Equity Association or similar union. These rules can include the frequency of washing, when new items are required, and requiring duplicates of some items to be made available. Be sure to confirm with your supervisor or the Stage Manager what union rules are in effect and be sure to familiarize yourself with the rules and confirm that you understand them prior to creating laundry paperwork.

If a production has multiple performances per week and will run for many weeks, creating a laundry schedule for all the costume pieces to ensure that they are all cleaned as often as necessary is very helpful. This will also expedite the process after performances, because the wardrobe crew members will know exactly what items to pull for laundry. Often "skins", which refers to costume pieces that touch the performers skin directly (for example, tights, undershirts, socks, dance belts, bras, underwear, etc.), are laundered after every performance. The same is true for costume pieces that get particularly sweaty during performances or end up stained due to something in the performance (for example, the use of fake blood or consumption of food onstage). Actor's Equity Association rules require (and industry best practices recommend) that two sets of "skins" are supplied for productions that will have two-show days, meaning a matinee and an evening performance on the same day. A two-show day often does not allow enough time between performances for laundry to be completed, especially hang drying, so having a second set of "skins" available for performers is helpful. On a two-show day, particularly sweaty items that cannot be laundered can be put in the dryer to freshen the items and dry the sweat, so that performers are not putting on wet clothes for the second performance. Items that cannot be dried can be hung on drying racks or hangers and placed over box fans to dry them as much as possible before the second performance.

Washing costume pieces as often as possible to keep them clean, fresh, and pleasant-smelling without overwhelming the wardrobe crew with laundry duties post-show is a delicate balancing act. Figure 3.7 shows an excerpt from a laundry schedule developed by Lucinda Koenig at The Phoenix Theatre Company. Each day has assigned garments to be washed according to color, so that the loads will all contain like colors. The full document contains a column for every day of the week when performances are held and an additional column with the garments that need to be sent to dry cleaning. The

TUESDAY			WEDNESDAY			THURSDAY	
Black			**White**			**Blue**	
Actor 9	1.4 Black Pleather Leggings (HW/DF)		Actor 13	1.4 White/Grey Stripe Shirt (MW/TDL)		Actor 3	1.4 Blue Cubs Hoodie (MW/TDL)
Actor 11	1.5 Black Pants (MW/TDL) OR (DC)		Actor 10	1.5 White/Blue Stripe Shirt (MW/TDL)		Actor 1	1.4 Turquoise Hijab (HW/HD)
Actor 13	1.6 Black Mock Turtle Neck (MW/TDL)		Actor 3	1.5 White/Black Sunburst Shirt (MW/TDL)		Actor 5	1.5 Light Blue Uniform Shirt (MW/TDL)
Actor 13	1.6 Black/Navy Tactical Pants (MW/TDL)		Actor 3	1.5 White/Grey Stripe Shirt (MW/TDL)		Actor 11	1.5 Blue Sweater Rig (MW/TDL)
Actor 3	1.6 Black Mock Turtle Neck (MW/TDL)		Actor 2	1.4 White Shirt (MW/TDL)		Actor 10	1.5 Blue Argyle Sweater Vest (HW/DF)
Actor 3	1.6 Black/Navy Tactical Pants (MW/TDL)		Actor 17	1.5 White Blouse (GW/TDL)		Actor 2	1.5 Light Blue Uniform Shirt (MW/TDL)
Actor 1	1.6 Black/White Smock (HW/DF)		Actor 7	1.4 White Turtle Neck (GW/TDL)		Actor 2	1.5 Navy Pants (GW/TDL or HD)
Actor 5	1.10 Black/Cream Stripe Cardigan (HW/DF)		Actor 8	1.4 White Sleeveless Shirt (GW/TDL)		Actor 9	1.5 Navy Suit Pants (MW/TDL)
Actor 3	1.10 Black Jeans (MW/TDL)		Actor 17	1.4 White Knee Socks (GW/TDL)		Actor 9	1.5 Navy Suit Jacket (MW/TDL)
Actor 5	1.4 Black Pants (MW/TDL)		Actor 14	1.4 White/Black Stripe Tee (MW/TDL)		Actor 7	1.5 Navy Dress (HW/HD)
Actor 3	1.8 Black Pants (MW/TDL)		Actor 17	1.6 White Pants (MW/TDL)		Actor 1	1.9 Navy Sparkles (MW/TDL)
Actor 3	1.9 Black Pants (MW/TDL)		Actor 6	1.6 White Sweater (MW/TDL)		Actor 8	1.5 Navy Skirt (MW/TDL)
Actor 3	2.6 Black Sweater (MW/TDL)		Actor 5	1.9 White Shirt (MW/TDL)		Actor 8	1.5 Navy Sweater Rig w/Stripe Shirt (MW/DF)
Actor 9	2.6 Black Skirt (MW/TDL)		Actor 11	1.9 White/Blue Stripe Shirt (MW/TDL)		Actor 13	1.9 Blue/Pink Stripe Shirt (MW/TDL)
Actor 6	1.9 Black Turtle Neck (GW/HD)		Actor 10	1.8 White Shirt (MW/TDL)		Actor 13	2.4 Navy Pants (MW/TDL)
Actor 6	1.9 Black Leggings (GW(io)/TDL)		Actor 3	1.9 White/Lavender Plaid Shirt (MW/TDL)		Actor 5	2.4 Blue/White Stripe Shirt (MW/TDL)
Actor 8	2.6 Black/Multi Graphic Leggings (MW/TDL or HD)		Actor 2	1.10 White Henley (MW/TDL)		Actor 11	1.9 Navy Pants (MW/TDL)
Actor 1	1.4 Black Leggings (GW/TDL)		Actor 21	1.5 White Blouse (GW/TDL)		Actor 11	2.4 Blue Sweater Vest (HW/DF)
Actor 1	1.5 Black Cardigan (GW/DF)		Actor 22	1.5 White Shirt (MW/TDL)		Actor 10	1.4 Navy Pants (MW/TDL)
Actor 1	2.4 Black Blazer (GW/HD)		Actor 22	1.8 White/Blue Stripe Shirt (MW/TDL)		Actor 10	1.6 Navy/Orange Islanders Sweatshirt (MW/TDL)
Actor 14	1.4 Black Leggings (GW/TDL)		Actor 15	1.5 White Collared Blouse (MW/TDL)		Actor 10	2.4 Blue/Green Argyle Sweater Vest (MW/TDL)
Actor 15	1.5 Black Slacks (GW(io)/TDL)		Actor 23	1.6 White Shirt (MW/TDL)		Actor 3	1.9 Blue/White Cloud Shirt (MW/TDL)
Actor 15	1.8 Black/White Print Pants (MW/TDL)		Actor 12	1.9 White/Blue Stripe Shirt (MW/TDL)		Actor 3	1.9 Navy Cardigan (MW/TDL)
Actor 15	2.3 Black Turtle Neck (GW/TDL)		Actor 18	1.4 White LS Epic Tee (MW/TDL)		Actor 3	1.10 Blue Winter Sweater (HW/DF)
Actor 16	2.2 Black Embroidered Dress (HW/HD)		Actor 19	1.5 White Mountains Tee (GW/TDL)		Actor 3	2.4 Blue Plaid Shirt (MW/TDL)
			Actor 22	2.3 White Legends Tee (MW/TDL)		Actor 2	1.9 Blue/White/Tan Stripe Shirt (MW/TDL)
			Actor 20	1.5 White Mountains Tee (GW/TDL)		Actor 2	2.6 Blue Michigan Hoodie (MW/TDL)
			Actor 13	2.1 White Gloves (MW/TDL)		Actor 9	1.6 Navy/Multi Print Leggings (GW/TDL)
Grey			Actor 2	2.4 White/Green/Blue Stripe Shirt (MW/TDL)		Actor 9	1.10 Teal Long Sleeve Tunic (MW/TDL)
Actor 6	1.4 Grey/Leather Dress (GW/HD)		Actor 17	2.7 Petticoat (MW/TDL)		Actor 6	1.6 Blue Pants (MW/TDL)
Actor 8	1.6 Grey Rainbow Stripe Sweatshirt (MW/TDL)		Actor 6	2.4 White/Blue Stripe Shirt (GW/TDL)		Actor 6	2.4 Navy Ruffle Skirt (MW/HD) OR (DC)
Actor 13	1.9 Grey Pants (MW/TDL)		Actor 8	2.4 White Blouse (MW/HD)		Actor 8	1.9 Blue Sweater Rig w/White Shirt (GW(io)/DF)
Actor 17	1.10 Grey Bird Sweatshirt (MW/TDL)					Actor 8	1.10 Blue/Orange Multi Stripe Sweater (MW/DF)
Actor 7	1.10 Grey Heather Knee Socks (GW/TDL)					Actor 1	1.6 Teal Puffy Jacket (GW/TDL)
Actor 11	2.6 Camo Grey Pants (MW/TDL)					Actor 1	1.9 Teal Sweater (MW/DF)
Actor 3	2.4 Grey/Yellow Print Shirt (MW/TDL)					Actor 1	2.4 Blue Sleeveless Dress (GW/HD)
Actor 6	2.6 Grey NY Giants Sweater (GW/TDL)		**Green**			Actor 1	2.6 Blue/Multi Sweater (HW(io)/DF)
Actor 1	1.4 Grey Dress (GW/TDL) or (DC)		Actor 13	Jacket (GW/HD)		Actor 14	1.5 Navy/Tan Windowpane Dress (HW/DF) OR (DC)
Actor 18	2.6 Grey Jeans (MW/TDL)		Actor 7	Shorts (GW/HD)		Actor 19	1.9 Navy Sweater (GW/DF)
Actor 19	1.5 Grey Jeans (MW/TDL)		Actor 22	Jacket (GW/HD)		Actor 21	1.9 Blue Dress (GW/HD)
Actor 20	1.5 Grey Jeans (MW/TDL)			Shorts (GW/HD)		Actor 22	2.4 Blue/White Stripe Shirt (MW/TDL)
			Actor 10	Jacket (GW/HD)		Actor 16	1.10 Teal Corduroy Skirt (MW/TDL)
			Actor 3	Jacket (GW/HD)		Actor 23	1.6 Navy Pants (MW/TDL)
Green			Actor 1	Jacket (GW/HD)		Actor 24	2.4 Blue/Contrast Collar Shirt (MW/TDL)
Actor 17	Jacket (GW/HD)		Actor 22	Jacket (GW/HD)		Actor 19	1.7 Blue/Plaid Sweater Rig (MW/DF)
Actor 6	Shorts (GW/HD)		Actor 23	Jacket (GW/HD)		Actor 19	2.3 Blue/Teal Plaid Shirt (MW/TDL)
	Jacket (GW/HD)			Shorts (GW/HD)		Actor 20	1.4 Blue Stripe Tee (MW/TDL)
Actor 8	Shorts (GW/HD)		Actor 24	Jacket (GW/HD)		Actor 19	1.7 Navy Blazer (MW/TDL) *CC
Actor 14	Jacket (GW/HD)		Actor 20	Jacket (GW/HD)			
	Shorts (GW/HD)			Shorts (GW/HD)			
Actor 15	Jacket (GW/HD)						
	Shorts (GW/HD)						
Actor 2	Jacket (GW/HD)						
	Shorts (GW/HD)						

Figure 3.7 A laundry schedule sorted by days of the week and load color created by Lucinda Koenig for The Phoenix Theatre Company.

PAPERWORK   41

FRIDAY		SATURDAY		SUNDAY	
Pink		**Yellow**		**Denim**	
Actor 10	1.4 Pink/Purple Print Jacket (GW/TDL)	Actor 5	1.4 Cream/White Collar Shirt (MW/TDL)	Actor 13	1.10 Jeans (MW/TDL)
Actor 9	1.6 Fuchsia Sweater Tunic (MW/TDL)	Actor 5	1.6 Yellow Kung Fu Tee (MW/TDL)	Actor 5	1.6 Jeans (MW/TDL)
Actor 17	1.10 Pink Turtle Neck (GW/DF)	Actor 24	1.9 Yellow Shirt (GW/TDL)	Actor 11	1.10 Denim Shirt (MW/TDL)
Actor 1	1.10 Pink Plaid Leggings (MW/TDL)	Actor 16	1.10 Yellow Top (MW/TDL)	Actor 6	2.6 Denim Jeggings (GW(io)/TDL)
Actor 14	1.10 Fuchsia Pants (GW(io)/HD)	Actor 14	2.1 Gold Spankie (GW/HD)	Actor 10	1.6 Jeans (MW/TDL)
Actor 17	2.4 Fuchsia Ruffle Blouse (MW/TDL)			Actor 2	1.10 Jeans (MW(io)/TDL)
Actor 7	2.6 Pink Floral Blouse (MW/TDL)			Actor 17	1.5 Stretchy Jeans (MW/TDL)
		Brown		Actor 17	1.10 Jeans (MW/TDL)
		Actor 10	1.9 Brown/Grey Argyle Sweater (MW/TDL)	Actor 7	1.4 Denim Jeggings (GW(io)/TDL)
		Actor 5	1.10 Brown Jeans (MW/TDL)	Actor 7	2.6 Jeans (MW/TDL)
Purple		Actor 9	1.10 Brown Jeggings (GW(io)/TDL)	Actor 1	1.6 Jeans (MW(io)/TDL)
Actor 17	1.4 Purple/Pink Galaxy Leggings (MW/TDL)			Actor 14	1.6 Denim Jeggings (GW/TDL)
Actor 7	1.9 Lavender Stripe Dress (MW/TDL)			Actor 18	1.4 Jeans (MW/TDL)
Actor 1	1.10 Purple Cow Sweater (MW/TDL)	**Tan**		Actor 19	2.3 Jeans (MW/TDL)
Actor 14	1.9 Purple Dress (GW/TDL)	Actor 14	1.5 Tan Cardigan (GW/TDL)	Actor 20	2.3 Jeans (MW/TDL)
Actor 8	2.4 Purple Sweater Vest (MW/DF)	Actor 11	1.9 Tan Coverall (MW/TDL)		
Actor 14	2.4 Purple Sweater (MW/TDL)	Actor 11	1.10 Tan Corduroy Pants (MW/TDL)		
		Actor 11	2.4 Khaki Pants (MW/TDL)	**Green**	
		Actor 15	2.3 Khaki Pants (GW/HD)	Actor 11	1.4 Green Cargo Pants (MW/TDL)
Red				Actor 3	1.4 Dark Olive Pants (MW/TDL)
Actor 25	1.1 Red Sweater (GW(io)/TDL)			Actor 7	1.6 Green Striped Sweater (HW/DF)
Actor 11	1.4 Red Cuba Tee (MW/TDL)	**Orange**		Actor 8	1.6 Green Polka Dot Pants (MW/TDL)
Actor 3	1.4 Red Santa Sweatshirt (MW/TDL)	Actor 13	1.4 Orange/Blue/Yellow Plaid Hoodie Combo (MW/TDL)	Actor 14	1.6 Lime Green Tee (GW/TDL)
Actor 3	1.4 Red Sweat Pants (MW/TDL)	Actor 10	1.9 Orange Pants (MW/TDL)	Actor 14	1.10 Lime Green Puffer Jacket (GW/HD)
Actor 8	1.6 Red Spankies (MW/TDL)	Actor 8	1.10 Orange Pants (MW(io)/TDL)	Actor 18	1.10 Green Christmas Tee (MW/TDL)
Actor 1	1.6 Red Petticoat (GW/HD)	Actor 7	2.4 Orange/Grey Dress (HW/HD)	Actor 19	1.10 Green Christmas Tee (MW/TDL)
Actor 17	1.6 Red Sparkies (MW/TDL)	Actor 13	2.4 White/Orange/Blue Plaid Shirt (MW/TDL)	Actor 20	1.10 Green Christmas Tee (MW/TDL)
Actor 6	1.6 Red/Green Argyle Sweater Vest (GW/TDL)	Actor 10	2.6 White/Red/Orange Plaid Shirt (MW/TDL)	Actor 14	2.1 Green Dress (HW/HD)
Actor 7	1.6 Red Sparkies (MW/TDL)	Actor 18	2.6 Orange Stripe Thermal (MW/TDL)	Actor 10	2.4 Lime Green Shirt (MW/TDL)
Actor 8	1.6 Red Sparkies (MW/TDL)			Actor 3	2.6 Green Pants (MW/TDL)
Actor 1	1.6 Red Sparkies (MW/TDL)			Actor 8	2.6 Green Sweater (MW(io)/TDL)
Actor 14	1.6 Red Sparkies (MW/TDL)			Actor 19	2.6 Green Stripe Thermal (MW/TDL)
Actor 16	1.6 Red Sparkies (MW/TDL)			Actor 13	1.6 Green Elf Tunic (HW/LD)
Actor 17	1.9 Maroon Blouse (HW/HD) OR (DC)			Actor 14	1.6 Green Elf Pants (HW/LD)
Actor 7	1.10 Red Christmas Sweater (GW(io)/DF)			Actor 5	1.6 Green Elf Tunic (HW/LD)
Actor 11	1.9 Burgundy Sweater (HW/HD)			Actor 5	1.6 Green Elf Pants (HW/LD)
Actor 23	1.6 Red/Green Argyle Sweater Vest (GW/TDL)			Actor 11	1.6 Green Elf Tunic (HW/LD)
Actor 19	1.4 Red Stripe Tee (MW/TDL)			Actor 11	1.6 Green Elf Pants (HW/LD)
Actor 15	1.5 Maroon Sweater (HW/HD)			Actor 10	1.6 Green Elf Tunic (HW/LD)
Actor 11	2.4 Red/Green/Blue Plaid Shirt (GW/TDL)			Actor 10	1.6 Green Elf Pants (HW/LD)
Salvan H	2.4 Red Christmas Sweater (MW/DF)			Actor 3	1.6 Green Elf Tunic (HW/LD)
Actor 5	2.6 Red/Blue Plaid Shirt (MW/TDL)			Actor 3	1.6 Green Elf Pants (HW/LD)
Actor 11	2.6 Burgundy Sweater (HW/DF)			Actor 3	1.6 Green Elf Tunic (HW/LD)
Actor 10	2.6 Burgundy Hoodie (MW/TDL)			Actor 3	1.6 Green Elf Pants (HW/LD)
Actor 10	2.6 Burgundy Pants (MW/TDL)			Actor 2	1.6 Green Elf Tunic (HW/LD)
Actor 19	2.6 Red Plaid Shirt (MW/TDL)			Actor 2	1.6 Green Elf Pants (HW/LD)
				Actor 9	1.6 Green Elf Dress w/attached red petticoat (HW/LD)
				Actor 17	1.6 Green Elf Dress (HW/LD)
				Actor 6	1.6 Green Elf Dress w/attached red petticoat (HW/LD)
				Actor 7	1.6 Green Elf Dress w/attached red petticoat (HW/LD)
				Actor 8	1.6 Green Elf Dress w/attached red petticoat (HW/LD)
				Actor 1	1.6 Green Elf Dress w/attached red petticoat (HW/LD)
				Actor 14	1.6 Green Elf Dress w/attached red petticoat (HW/LD)
				Actor 16	1.6 Green Elf Dress w/attached red petticoat (HW/LD)

Figure 3.7 *(Continued)*

			Dry Clean		
Actor 13	1.4 Black Slacks		Actor 9	1.4 White Sleeveless Ruffle Blouse	Actor 22	1.5 Navy Suit Pants
Actor 13	1.5 Grey Jacket		Actor 9	1.9 Tan Suit Jacket	Actor 22	1.5 Naby Suit Jacket
Actor 13	1.9 Navy Jacket		Actor 9	1.9 Tan Suit Pants	Actor 22	1.8 Grey Suit Pants
Actor 13	1.10 Brown/Blue Stripe Sweater		Actor 9	1.9 Blue Blouse	Actor 22	1.8 Grey Suit Jacket
Actor 13	2.1 Santa Jacket		Actor 9	2.6 Red Wool Jacket	Actor 12	1.8 Grey Suit Jacket
Actor 13	2.1 Santa Pants		Actor 17	1.5 Tan Pants	Actor 12	1.1 Cozy Santa Pants
Actor 5	1.4 Grey Sport Coat		Actor 17	1.9 Black Jacket	Actor 25	2.5 Formal Santa Pants
Actor 5	1.9 Blue Stripe Jacket		Actor 17	1.9 Black Pants	Actor 25	2.5 Santa Jacket
Actor 5	2.1 Santa Jacket		Actor 17	2.4 Grey Suit Jacket	Actor 25	1.6 Grey Sport Coat
Actor 5	2.1 Santa Pants		Actor 17	2.4 Grey Suit Pants	Matravius	2.1 Santa Jacket
Actor 11	2.1 Santa Jacket		Actor 17	END Mrs. Claus Dress	Matravius	2.1 Santa Coat
Actor 11	2.1 Santa Pants		Actor 7	1.9 Navy Blazer	Scott	1.9 Navy Suit Jacket
Actor 10	1.8 Black Jacket w/Gold Buttons		Actor 8	1.4 Navy/Purple Plaid Skirt	Scott	1.9 Navy Suit Pants
Actor 10	2.1 Santa Pants		Actor 8	1.9 Grey/Navy Skirt	Scott	2.4 Grey Suit Jacket
Actor 10	2.1 Santa Jacket		Actor 8	2.4 Green Skirt	Scott	2.4 Grey Suit Vest
Actor 3	1.5 Grey Pants		Actor 14	2.4 Orange Print Skirt	Scott	2.4 Grey Suit Pants
Actor 3	1.5 Grey Vest		Anne-Lise	1.5 Black Tweed Skirt	Actor 20	1.7 Navy Blazer
Actor 3	1.9 Navy Pants		Anne-Lise	1.5 Black Tweed Jacket		
Actor 3	2.1 Santa Jacket		Anne-Lise	2.4 Orange Suit Skirt		
Actor 3	2.1 Santa Jacket		Anne-Lise	2.4 Orange Suit Jacket		
Actor 3	2.4 Tan Pants		Actor 15	1.8 White Sleeveless Blouse		
Actor 3	2.4 Purple Blazer		Actor 16	2.6 Purple Dress		
Actor 3	1.5 Grey Vest					
Actor 3	1.9 Grey/ Lavender Back Vest					
Actor 3	2.1 Santa Jacket					
Actor 3	2.1 Santa Pants	1.5 lbs	Suit Jacket (23) = 34.5 lbs			
Actor 2	1.4 Tan Suit Pants	1.5 lbs	Pants (16) = 24 lbs			
Actor 2	1.4 Tan Suit Jacket	0.3 lbs	Vest (4) = 1.2 lbs			
Actor 2	2.1 Santa Jacket	1.0 lbs	Skirt (6) = 6.0 lbs			
Actor 2	2.1 Santa Pants	2.0 lbs	Dress (1) = 2.0 lbs			
Actor 2	1.9 Blue Suit Jacket	0.5 lbs	Blouse (3) = 1.5 lbs			
Actor 2	1.9 Blue Suit Pants	1.0 lbs	Sweater (1) = 1.0 lbs			
Actor 2	2.4 Grey Suit Pants	1.0 lbs	Overcoat (1) = 1.0 lbs			
Actor 2	2.4 Grey Suit Jacket	1.5 lbs	Santa Jacket (8) = 12.0 lbs			
		1.5 lbs	Santa Pants (8) = 12.0 lbs			
		9.0 lbs	Mr. & Mrs. Claus Looks (4pcs) = 9.0 lbs			
			Total Estimated Weight = 104.2 lbs			

Figure 3.7 *(Continued)*

abbreviations indicate the laundry care instructions for the garment (for example, MW/TDL = machine wash/tumble dry low). This schedule not only ensures that all costume pieces are washed or dry cleaned once per week but only requires two to three loads per night. Hand-washing tasks were generally reserved for Sundays, which tended to take place after matinee performances with the day off being Monday, so items would have enough time to dry before Tuesday evening's performance.

Dry cleaning is a huge consideration for wardrobe professionals. If you work for a resident company, establishing a relationship with a local dry cleaner who may offer you a discount based on the volume and frequency of your usage, but can also get the costumes cleaned between a Sunday evening and Tuesday early evening, is imperative. It is also important to talk with local dry cleaners about the types of items you may be bringing in and what types of items they cannot service. I learned that different dry cleaners use different types of solvents, and some of them will damage rhinestones and sequins. You may even need to have two different dry cleaners, one that you take all your regular dry cleaning to and one that services specialty items. In a pinch, the at-home dry cleaning kits that can be used in the dryer are better than not cleaning items at all, but professional dry-cleaning service is recommended.

When creating laundry paperwork, it is important to know the washing instructions for each costume piece and make a note of it. Store-bought items will often have washing instructions on their tag. Some items may not have instructions, so use your best judgment. If you are concerned something should not get wet, it may be best to send it to the dry cleaner. You should consult the costume team who built the costume pieces about washing instructions for any newly built items. Hopefully they will know how the fabric was prewashed and how the garment can best be cared for. Try not to send items that do not need to be dry cleaned to the dry cleaner, if handwashing or the gentle cycle are a possibility, because dry-cleaning costs can add up quickly.

The laundry schedule and additional laundry paperwork help the wardrobe team ensure that all costumes are maintained properly and cleaned regularly. Sharing this paperwork with the costume department is beneficial in case the costume pieces are reused in future productions.

The paperwork samples provided in this chapter are a wonderful starting point as you begin to create wardrobe paperwork. The most important thing is to do what works for you, your team, and the needs of your production. Experimenting with different formats and ways of documenting things until you find what works best for you will be the key to success with your wardrobe paperwork. Hopefully you understand the importance of creating wardrobe paperwork and documenting the details of running the show. Paperwork helps prevent mistakes, ensures accuracy, promotes consistency, and creates a record in case of new personnel coming onboard during the run of a show. Paperwork can also be utilized if a production is remounted in the future, which will save the next wardrobe team from having to start from scratch. The power of paperwork cannot be overstated.

CHAPTER 4

Being a Team Leader

RUNNING YOUR CREW

Running wardrobe can be stressful for all involved, so it is important for the Wardrobe Supervisor to be an effective leader. Individuals will employ various leadership techniques and strategies, but there are a few things that all good leaders have in common. Excellent organization, clear communication, and effective delegation are a few elements that contribute to success. As the inevitable chaos of a backstage environment during tech rehearsals and performances unfolds, a calm and confident wardrobe supervisor can make all the difference.

To employ excellent organization, it is important to have as much information as you can prior to the beginning of the tech process and attempt to solve problems and have a game plan in place. Setting up backstage areas and labeling everything clearly will help your crew know where to find things. Designating specific places for all items will cut down on time spent looking for lost pieces. Preemptive planning with other departments about the wardrobe department's need for backstage changing areas and spaces to store costume items will help set you up for success. Creating wardrobe paperwork with all available information and assigning crew members to specific tracks will help avoid confusion about who is doing what. Sometimes knowing that things will continuously change throughout the tech process is frustrating and causes wardrobe supervisors to hesitate about creating paperwork. I encourage you to draft as much paperwork as possible for your crew, knowing that it will change but that even having an outline is better than having nothing to start with. Following up with costume designers and shop staff to try to get questions answered prior to tech will also help resolve potential issues.

This leads to communication. One mistake that wardrobe supervisors often make is hoarding information to themselves out of insecurity. People think that if they are the only ones that know something, it makes them more valuable, and they equate that with job security. Unfortunately, when you are a supervisor, withholding information from your team actually hinders the process for everyone and makes you a less effective leader. If it were possible for the wardrobe supervisor to run the entire production themselves, the organization would not hire additional wardrobe crew personnel. For crew members to feel ownership of their tasks, they need all the information communicated to them. This is the first step in effective delegation. I often refer to this aspect of leadership as "if I get hit by a bus", but the reality is that anything could happen to any one of us at any time. If an individual hoards information and does not distribute it to their team or anyone else in their organization and something happens to them, the entire production and all of the personnel involved suffer.

I recommend keeping your paperwork on a share-drive of some sort and ensuring that your crew, the stage management team, the costume staff, and production management all have access to it. Make full dressing lists, costume plots, and run sheets available to your entire crew. They may not all need to know what everyone in the cast is wearing at any given time, but if they need to double-check something, it is good for them to have that access. This does not diminish your importance in the least; it actually makes you an extraordinarily effective manager that communicates effectively with the team. Do not underestimate the power of communicating with your team. If you get dressing notes from the costume designer, share them with your team in addition to the performers. Dressing notes refer to a correction that is made about how something was worn (or not worn) onstage. That way they can make sure the notes are fixed for the next performance and avoid future problems. If the designer changes something, make sure the entire wardrobe crew knows so that they don't get confused when they see something different. Open lines of communication are one of the most important contributors to the success of a wardrobe crew and that communication comes from the supervisor.

Communication is the first step to effective delegation. You can't do this alone, even though many wardrobe supervisors seem like superheroes who can multitask with the best of them. The more you can delegate tasks to your crew instead of always saying, "I'll take care of it", the more you will be free to actually supervise. If you are always doing the most complicated quick-changes yourself, how can you take care of a costume emergency that arises mid-show? What if you assigned your most experienced crew member to the complicated quick-change, but could be nearby in case anything went awry on a given day? If you are doing a quick costume piece repair mid-show and something else goes wrong, who is left to deal with it? Can anyone on your crew make that repair, leaving you free to deal with other issues that may arise? Making yourself the default person to do everything, handle everything, and supervise everything is not a realistic way to run a crew. Additionally, crew members perform better when they feel their role is important. If they are performing the toughest changes, making mid-show repairs, and prepping costumes for the leading actor, they will be more invested in their job. I encourage you to be mindful about delegating as much as possible, which in turn empowers your team and protects you from burnout.

As you begin to improve your delegation skills, you will begin to realize that not every task can be delegated to every person. An important part of management is understanding the strengths and weaknesses of your team members and setting them up for success as much as possible. If you have a new wardrobe crew member, try to assess their skills and give them a track with less responsibility than that of your most experienced person. Hopefully everyone on your team is good at something. Some people are great at pre-show tasks like steaming and pressing and presets. Others are really great at quick-changes and staying calm under pressure. A few might be best at post-show duties such as check-in, spraying, and laundry. Maybe someone is very adept at working with difficult personalities backstage. Trying to coordinate your crew's assignments with their strengths will set them up for success and contribute to a positive atmosphere backstage. Great wardrobe supervisors create tracks for their crew that they know they can handle and take ownership of. This also demonstrates very effective delegation.

WORKING WITH PERFORMERS

Establishing a positive relationship with performers is a key skill for those who work in wardrobe. For this section, I interviewed a long-time colleague of mine who is a New York City-based performer and arts educator with over 20 years of experience, John Anker Bow. John has spent many years performing in various venues and situations, including many national tours. He has worked with hundreds of different wardrobe people on many productions, so I wanted to find out from him what makes the dynamic between performers and the wardrobe team work best. As we know, there is a tendency among creative types (of all job descriptions) to be dramatic. Having a wardrobe supervisor who remains calm and communicates in a clear, concise, and professional manner helps to create balance in this relationship. The wardrobe team must also convey organization and understanding, which helps performers to feel more at ease. Wardrobe, hair, and makeup personnel interact with performers on a very personal level, much more so than others on the crew, so it is important to try to make the performers comfortable with the people in these roles. Wardrobe work often necessitates physical interaction between wardrobe crew members and performers. It is important to respect everyone's bodily autonomy and ensure that performers feel safe, secure, and that they have control over their own physical self. Acknowledge that some areas or types of contact may be triggering or sensitive for people (such as

Figure 4.1 A student wardrobe supervisor and crew member rehearse a quick-change with a performer backstage at Albright College.
Photograph taken by John Pankratz, Ph.D.

hair/hats, undergarments, etc.) and act from a place of empathy, compassion, and understanding. Always explain what you are going to do before doing it and ask permission if something necessitates physical contact. Working with performers to establish actions and a routine with which they and the crew members feel comfortable and safe is an important function of the wardrobe supervisor. Figure 4.1 depicts wardrobe crew members discussing a quick-change with a performer during a dress rehearsal.

How can you create a positive dynamic with performers? Communicate expectations early, both for your team and for the company. What is the laundry schedule? When will costumes be available pre-show? Who is taking care of quick-changes and how will they be rehearsed? How would you like performers to communicate notes about repairs or issues with your team? Establishing procedures, schedules, expectations, and information early in the process will help performers feel comfortable with how you will operate as a Wardrobe Supervisor. If something changes or deviates from the schedule for any reason, let the performers know. It will be much easier for them to understand why something is different if it is communicated in advance with sound reasoning and not sprung on them at the last minute.

Due to the personal nature of wardrobe work, performers may come to you with issues or problems and sometimes it is something that is causing them a great deal of stress. Although you should not tolerate disrespect, it is helpful to try to understand what performers are trying to communicate to you or your crew members, even if they are not saying it in the most gracious way at all times. If there is a small accommodation that can be made to make a performer more comfortable, you should try to honor the request if at all possible. If wardrobe personnel go above and beyond for a performer, particularly in a stressful time, it can have a huge impact and truly mean the world to the performer. Try to establish and maintain an open line of communication with performers so they feel comfortable sharing problems or concerns with you. Be honest and upfront about your priorities and workload so that performers understand why a particular issue may not be addressed immediately. People are generally empathetic and understanding, but only if they are given enough information to understand the situation. Wardrobe teams are often dealing with massive amounts of requests, repairs, and show maintenance, but not everyone realizes everything on the to-do list every day. Being transparent with your communication and promising only what you know you can deliver will help performers to trust you and feel confident that you are listening to them and attempting to help however you can.

Establishing a rapport with performers can lead to the issue of being too social backstage during performances. Let's face it, many who work in this industry are fun, outgoing, and interesting to talk to. This can lead to a great backstage atmosphere, but it can be problematic if it distracts from the work at hand. It is best to focus on the work first and engage in conversation second. Make sure you finish the quick-change, hand the performer their water bottle so they can get a drink before returning to stage, and then chat for a few seconds if you have time and the performer seems eager to do so. If you are working on a local wardrobe crew, sometimes you are only with the show for three to five performances. It is fun to get to know new people, but you also need to learn your track and execute it quickly and efficiently as there is no rehearsal time and your first try is a live performance. The best approach is to focus completely on the show in the first performance, solidify your routine in the second performance, and then chit chat where appropriate for the remaining performances if others seem eager to do so. If you are working on a performance that is a one-nighter, focus on the changes going smoothly above all else. Finding the balance between socializing backstage and executing your tasks perfectly is a skill that comes with practice, but focusing more heavily on the work is always a good default.

Speaking of focusing on the work, cell phones, smart watches, and other tech items have become an issue for people backstage. If a performer is running to you for a quick-change and you are scrolling on your phone, it doesn't appear that work is your priority. Sometimes your track has large amounts of downtime, so it may be appropriate to check your phone, but be sure that all possible work tasks are accomplished first. Also check that your phone is on silent mode and can't light up or make noise at inappropriate times backstage. Sometimes the rule is no phones on the deck (backstage) at all. If this is the rule somewhere you are working, abide by it.

As a wardrobe supervisor with a production, it is important to anticipate problems and be proactive about solutions. This is particularly true during the tech process, as it can be very fast-paced, and details can be difficult to manage. Try to get as clear a picture as possible of the whole show, from beginning to end. The better you know the show, the easier time you will have answering questions and planning your next move. Every job you do can be a learning experience, but you want to be the one who is helpful, calm, and solves problems as much as possible. Sometimes I compare being a wardrobe supervisor to being a firefighter. In this case, the more "extinguishers" you can have pre-set and ready to deploy, the better. Tech and live performance can be stressful but try to be conscious of your tone to not add to the stress of the situation. Don't blow things out of proportion and try not to be condescending, even if someone has made a mistake. We all make mistakes and keeping a positive attitude will help those around you feel comfortable as they try to improve. Try your best not to get involved with any petty disputes or gossip that can sometimes crop up backstage. This will do nothing but distract you from your work and cause unnecessary tension and worry.

Remember that when it comes to live performance, we are all on the same team. Without any single member of the cast or crew doing their job, the show would not go on. Although it can sometimes be a pressure cooker of stress, tempers, deadlines, and challenges, we do this job because we love it, and we can't imagine doing anything else. Even on the worst days, it is nice to know that we are part of a community that supports each other, and everyone truly wants to see each other succeed. There is no greater high than opening a show and being proud of the work you and your team did to make it all run smoothly. Fostering positive relationships with performers will make your job that much more rewarding and give you a more positive work environment. This will also give your crew higher morale and contribute to a better experience for all involved. Honing your interpersonal skills is an important part of your success as a wardrobe supervisor.

CREATING AN INCLUSIVE BACKSTAGE ATMOSPHERE

The backstage environment can vary greatly from production to production. The good news is that as a wardrobe supervisor, you have a lot of influence on what that atmosphere is like. The most important thing is that the backstage environment feels safe for everyone. This can mean a lot of things: Everyone treats each other with mutual respect, the area is free from obvious hazards and safety concerns, problems can be discussed and solved, and individual identity is esteemed. Interpersonal issues can certainly arise, but it is important for the wardrobe supervisor to act professionally and try to maintain positive relationships with everyone backstage. The wardrobe supervisor should be approachable so that concerns can be voiced and hopefully solutions can be negotiated. If you are going to spend a lot of your professional career backstage, you want the backstage atmosphere to be positive. If you dread going to work every day, that is not going to lead to a fulfilling experience.

Talking to performers about their preferred dressing room assignments and coordinating that with stage management is very important. There are sometimes union or contractual rules about dressing rooms, so you shouldn't switch anything without discussing the change with the stage management team and possibly production management if there is a larger question. If there are items that performers need in their dressing rooms or backstage to make them more comfortable, it is good to provide them (if possible and within reason). Dressing rooms are often assigned according to gender binary. Traditionally, there have been such things as male chorus and female chorus dressing rooms. As the industry strives to be more inclusive, this is an area that needs to change. Everyone should feel comfortable with their dressing room assignment, regardless of their gender identity. I have seen this addressed successfully by removing male and female signage and posting signs that say "this bathroom has urinals" or "this bathroom has toilets", inviting people to use the bathroom of their choosing. Often, the stage manager will establish the dressing room assignments because they are more familiar with the dynamics of the cast. However, if you are tasked with this and are unsure of where to assign a particular performer, I recommend asking them where they would feel most comfortable. It is also important to make sure there is a private space that cast members can dress in if they choose. Often this can be a bathroom stall located in or close to the dressing room. Performers have different levels of modesty, and it is important to be respectful of everyone. As a wardrobe professional, you may need to enter the dressing rooms when performers are changing or getting dressed. It is standard practice to knock on the door, announce yourself as wardrobe, and wait for someone inside to give you the okay to enter. You may find some performers who are uncomfortable with wardrobe people entering the dressing rooms. It is important to make it clear that all of the items inside the dressing room are a part of the wardrobe crew's professional responsibilities, and they will need access to them. When entering an occupied dressing room, crew members should be efficient about what they need to do and exit the room quickly. They should try not to look at people in the room unless they have entered to speak to a performer about something costume-related and urgent. Trying to perform as many tasks as possible that involve entering the dressing rooms prior to the arrival of cast members and only entering them once they have arrived if absolutely necessary will contribute to the comfortability of all involved. It is important to note here that Actor's Equity Association guidelines as well as good professional practice require that juvenile performers be given a separate dressing space from adults.

Mutual respect is important and is often a part of the culture of a particular organization or production. Hopefully, you will find yourself working in settings where crew members are treated well by the cast and other company members. If you find this is not the case, it is best to try to mitigate bad behavior as early as possible. Talk to the stage management team, the director, the artistic director, the production manager, or anyone who you feel will understand your concerns and work with you to find a solution. At the collegiate level, my department works to emphasize the value of all members of the company, which includes cast, crew, front of house, artistic, production, and more.

If you or your crew members are being treated with disrespect, try not to get angry and escalate the situation, especially if it is during a performance. Generally, talking with those involved after the situation has deescalated and everyone has a chance to cool off will lead to more positive outcomes. If you are addressing disrespect with someone, try not to sound accusatory, and remember that there are three sides to every story (yours, mine, and the truth). Calmly express the impact of the behavior and discuss what kind of changes will improve the situation. Listen to any concerns from both sides and try to negotiate a solution that works for everyone. Remind your crew members (and others) that you don't have to like everyone or be best friends with them, but you do have to act professionally and be courteous to one another, especially during stressful situations. One of the most important things for everyone backstage to try to do is not take things personally. If a quick-change is going awry and someone yells at someone else, it is because they are stressed and frustrated, not because they are intentionally trying to hurt the other person's feelings. This is not an excuse for bad behavior, especially on a consistent basis, but live production work requires the understanding that everyone can have a bad day and sometimes people react in a way they aren't proud of. Extending grace and understanding to those around you will go a long way in promoting a positive backstage experience and preventing hurt feelings.

Sometimes you may need to address a performer who is unwilling to wear a particular costume piece or accessory or is wearing it differently than the costume designer intended. Hopefully there is enough dress rehearsal time that this can be addressed by the costume designer and the director if needed, but sometimes performers will change something after opening night, so it is left to the wardrobe supervisor to maintain the artistic vision of the costume designer. There are various ways you can approach this, and different solutions may work with different performers and situations. If you have a good rapport with the performer, sometimes asking them to do it as a favor to you is the easiest way to resolve the issue. Saying something such as "my job is to make sure that the costumes are worn when and how the costume designer intended, so if that is not happening, then it is my fault, and I can get in trouble" may reframe the situation and the performer may oblige. A reminder about chain of command and the theater's rules can also be helpful, such as "After opening night, we cannot change anything about the costume pieces or how they are worn per our contract with the designer". Offering a solution or compromise that does not affect the look of the costume piece can help resolve a problem. Shoes have become uncomfortable; can you offer an insole, heel grip, or a thinner sock? A scarf is irritating the neck; is there a different way to tie it that is more comfortable? They have been working out a lot and their pants are suddenly falling down; can you take them in a little bit or provide a belt or suspenders? Trying to work with performers to make them more comfortable while maintaining the costume designer's vision will go a long way toward a positive workplace. If these solutions are not working and the show has already opened, the first person to talk with is the stage manager. Hopefully you have a good working relationship with the stage manager, and maybe they have a better rapport with the performer and could have a positive outcome by having the conversation. Also letting the performer know that deviations from the costume design need to be included in the performance report may give a gentle reminder that future casting decisions could be impacted by their behavior. If you and the stage manager are unable to reach an acceptable outcome with the performer, you may need to consult the production manager or the artistic director for further assistance.

   Another aspect of a safe and positive backstage environment is addressing obvious safety concerns or hazards. If there isn't enough light backstage and cast and crew members are bumping into things and tripping, ask if more clip lights or running lights can be installed. If laundry baskets, racks, chairs, or other wardrobe items pose safety risks for others, try to find places for them that are out of the way or well-marked. If items get thrown around in a quick-change, try to clean them up and promptly clear the area so others don't trip over items in the dark. Being aware of the safety risks of backstage and trying your best to mitigate them is an important part of the wardrobe supervisor's work. Ensure that performers, your crew, and everyone backstage feel comfortable discussing any issues they may be having with you so that solutions can be found.

   Know that sometimes people will discuss issues with you that do not have a solution. Maybe an actor doesn't like their costume for a particular scene. Maybe a wardrobe crew member doesn't get along with someone backstage and is assigned to their side of the stage for all of Act 1. Maybe there is a personality backstage that rubs many people the wrong way. There may not always be a solution for a particular issue, but you do want people, especially your crew, to feel comfortable talking to you about things that come up. Sometimes it is just helpful to vent to someone and know that they are listening to and understand you. It also gives you a warning about potential larger issues, so if you can solve a small problem, you may be able to avoid big problems.

This is all part of making sure people are comfortable backstage. An inclusive and supportive backstage atmosphere allows performers to give their best onstage and crew members to enjoy their work. If anyone is being made to feel uncomfortable backstage for any reason, it is good practice to try to find a resolution.

Understanding the delicacy of certain conversations and respecting that it may be hard for someone to voice a particular concern helps to make you approachable. Try not to have sensitive conversations in large dressing rooms full of people or in the common areas where everyone is waiting backstage. If you notice a situation that seems tense or uncomfortable, make a note to check in with those involved after the performance. Being aware of the goings-on around you and how people are interacting will help you troubleshoot interpersonal issues as they arise. All of this said, you do want to establish boundaries for yourself and try to keep these conversations professional in nature. Live production can have relationships and dynamics that are not always professional. People spend long hours together and often spend time together outside of work as well. Sometimes members of a cast or crew may be dating, be best friends, be family, or otherwise have relationships that extend beyond the production. If you allow yourself to get dragged into every interpersonal conflict backstage, including those that are not exclusive to the production, you will be overwhelmed and unable to focus on the task at hand. Trying to address issues that seem production-related and professional in nature is a good place to start.

Creating a backstage environment where everyone feels respected, included, and safe is an important part of the wardrobe supervisor's job. Striving for performer and crew comfortability, maintaining open lines of communication, and listening to and addressing issues that arise will help you create a positive environment. Do not be afraid to seek assistance with issues you feel are important to address but are beyond the scope of your responsibilities, but also try to go the extra mile to help where you can. You will directly benefit from your efforts by working in a healthier, happier place.

COLLABORATING WITH STAGE MANAGEMENT

The stage management team and wardrobe team collaborate sporadically throughout the production process and consistently through tech rehearsals and performances. Promoting full communication and a positive work relationship with stage management is essential to the wardrobe supervisor's success. What types of information need to be communicated? How can you best collaborate with the stage management team? What do you need to know to be successful in tech rehearsals and performances?

Let's start with information and communication. Stage management keeps track of everything during the rehearsal process. Here are some items that might be of interest to the wardrobe supervisor:

1. Performers entrance and exit locations and times;
2. Which performers are in which scenes;
3. Things performers do that may affect wardrobe (remove costume pieces onstage, spill on themselves, high impact movements such as crawling on their knees for a duration, knee pad/safety needs, dance needs, special FX such as blood, etc.).

In turn, you may have some information that stage management needs to know, and the earlier you share it with them, the better. This part may involve collaboration with the Costume Designer or costume shop staff. If stage management knows that a performer has a quick-change during a song or scene, they can let the director know that the performer cannot be added into another scene during that time. If they know that a performer is wearing a cumbersome period dress with a hoop, they can ask if certain blocking will work. If they know all the actresses will be corseted, they can request corsets for dance rehearsals to ensure the choreography can be performed.

One thing that has made a big difference to wardrobe supervisors in working with stage management is asking them to make an entrance and exit chart to be provided at the crew watch (or designer run) (see Figure 2.1 in Chapter 2). This helps stage management track the movement of the performers throughout the show during rehearsals and allows the wardrobe supervisor to more easily time the quick-changes when they see a run-through for the first time. I have to thank the stage management team at The Phoenix Theatre Company for creating the template I have provided and for always creating a chart for designer run.

Be sure you are receiving rehearsal reports and production meeting minutes if you are the wardrobe supervisor for a production. Even though much of the information will not be relevant to you, it is good to stay in the loop and be aware of potential concerns well in advance of tech rehearsals. Don't be afraid to ask questions if something in the reports or minutes could be an issue. As you begin creating your paperwork, share your drafts with stage management so that they can let you know if anything looks incorrect or they have questions. Stage management is also a great resource regarding union rules. If you are working on an AEA (Actor's Equity Association) production or your company abides by any union rules for the performers or crew, the stage managers will likely have all the specific information about it. Checking in with them to ensure that wardrobe is complying with all mandates helps to avoid violations and repercussions. By working together with the stage management team and freely sharing information back and forth, many potential issues can be avoided or solved in advance.

If you are new to a company or production process, set up a meeting with the stage managers in advance to discuss the tech rehearsal process. Every company runs a little bit differently, and being familiar with the expectations beforehand helps to avoid confusion and keep things running smoothly. When are costumes added to the process? Sometimes they are worn from the very beginning of tech, while other times they are added when tech is completed and dress rehearsals begin. Is it OK to stop, rehearse, and run quick-changes during the rehearsal, or does the company prefer separate quick-change rehearsals to be scheduled beforehand? If a quick-change takes too long, do they want to stop and go back to get it right or keep going and go back to it later? What time do costumes need to be set for the rehearsal to begin? It is best not to assume anything, even if you have a lot of experience running wardrobe. Asking questions and clarifying the process and expectations beforehand will help you collaborate successfully with the stage management team.

If you have never done this before and aren't sure where to start, here is how I prefer to set this up. If there are tech rehearsals and cue-to-cue rehearsals that will focus on lighting, sound, and scenic elements, I prefer to not add costumes as it results in performers spending a lot of time standing around sweating under the lights. These rehearsals also do not give accurate timing for wardrobe, because they are often holding and going back to perfect scenic shifts and other cues. I like to add costumes for a first dress rehearsal once the show has been fully teched through by the other areas. During the first dress rehearsal, I ask performers to discuss their quick-changes ahead of time with the wardrobe crew member who will be performing the change. If it is not possible to discuss in advance, I ask stage management to hold prior to the quick-change so wardrobe and the performer can talk through it first. I then ask them to run the change in time with the scene. If the change runs smoothly, the rehearsal continues. If it does not, I ask for a hold (meaning everyone stops to await instruction) and the chance to adjust if needed and try again (maybe someone got stuck in their pants leg or didn't get handed their costume pieces in the right order or some other simple thing that can be fixed quickly). If the change is still not working, sometimes it is a larger issue that needs more time to be fixed (snaps swapped for Velcro™, shoes laced with elastic, or a closure changed to magnets). If this is the case, I write down the note and the rehearsal continues. We would then schedule a quick-change rehearsal for the next day after the adjustment can be made to the costume. Assistant Stage Managers are often on headsets backstage, so it is important to coordinate with them if you are going to be calling a hold or asking to run a change again. They can communicate via headset with the Stage Manager to make sure everyone knows what is going on and keep the rehearsal running smoothly. Do not hold or repeat a quick-change without the OK from your stage management team or deck manager. You do not want to be blamed for holding up a dress rehearsal because of poor communication or because of confusion. This is extraordinarily important. Alec Ferrell, an AEA production stage manager, had this to say, "Time is always at a premium and Stage Management is trying to balance out the needs of the many, and time is the currency. Being able to know when to re-run a quick-change or to take notes and address [it] later is paramount. It is also important to understand that [stage management] is weighing it all out, so it is not a personal slight if a costume note can't be addressed in the moment. They will find the time with wardrobe [by] working together".

Throughout the performances, it is important to continue communicating with your stage management team. If something goes wrong on a particular night, you should let them know what happened and what the solution is so that it doesn't happen again. If it is mid-performance and an emergency arises, your communication needs to be immediate, clear, concise, and honest. The stage management team is your first line of support when something goes wrong. They may want to include this information in the performance report, so they will need to get the details from you. If a costume piece needs extreme repair or replacement, that may also go in the report (and you should communicate it directly to the costume shop manager). The Stage Manager also sees the show from a different vantage point and can sometimes observe if things about a costume don't look right. A performer's dress is sliding down in the dance number, does it need to be taken in a little bit? A performer enters from their quick-change looking unintentionally disheveled, did something go wrong? These are just a couple of examples of observations stage managers might make by seeing the show from the front. Don't take any of their feedback as criticism, they are simply sharing observations and information that may be helpful to you to keep the show looking its' best.

The stage management team will communicate information with the wardrobe team about understudies and swings. If your production has understudies and swings, be sure to clarify how you will know who is in or out for a given performance and when that information will be available. Also discuss what happens in the case of an emergency, maybe when a performer does not show up at a half-hour call. Would the opening time for the house need to be adjusted? You want to consider all factors and potential needs for an emergency situation and formulate a plan because during the emergency is not a good time to come up with the plan.

The stage management team are key collaborators with the wardrobe team. Establishing open communication and the flow of information between the two is essential to the success of the production. Coordinating with stage management about the dress rehearsal process will help keep things running efficiently and clarifying expectations for each area throughout the production process will cut down on surprises and things falling through the cracks.

CHAPTER 5

Tools and Safety

SAFETY AND THE PARAMETERS OF THE JOB

One thing that can come as a surprise to people is how physically demanding wardrobe and costume work can be. I don't know about you, but when I tell people what I do for work, a common reaction is "Oh, that must be so fun". This used to infuriate me, because I took it as an insult. I felt like they meant that my work is easy and always fun. As anyone who works in the live performance industry can tell you, there are a lot of moments when our jobs are far from fun. I no longer get infuriated when I hear this, I have come to realize that I am fortunate to have a career doing something that I love to do, even if there are times when the work is challenging, frustrating, and stressful. I take great pride in having a successful career and I'm thankful for the many opportunities I have had up until this point and I look forward to what lies ahead for me professionally.

All that said, my career has also taken its toll on me physically. I am not a medical professional or a fitness expert, but I try to learn as much as I can about how to keep myself in shape so that I can continue to work in this field as I age. Personally, I have knee and lower back problems, and a mild case of asthma that is mostly exercise- and heat-induced. Why am I telling you this? Because it is important to be aware of issues with your own body to make sure you can keep yourself safe and avoid injury when working in wardrobe. Costumes are heavy, and we are often carrying as many as we can lift as quickly as we can in low light or other treacherous conditions. When working a load-out with a tight timeline, you may be tempted to lift more than you are safely able to save time. Do not do that. A back injury takes a very long time to recover from and many people with back injuries end up with chronic back problems and chronic pain that makes this kind of work all the more difficult. Also, do not run at work, especially in the dark. Have I done it? Yes, twice that I can remember vividly. Once I was able to retrieve the forgotten costume piece from the dressing room in time and get it on the performer prior to their entrance. And then I had an asthma attack backstage and had to have my inhaler administered to me. Was it worth it to get a hat onstage? Had I double-checked the performer sooner I may have been able to avoid running back to the dressing room in a full sprint. The other time, I ran full speed up a spiral, metal staircase frantically looking for a forgotten costume piece in the loft dressing room. I eventually found it but did not make it back in time and the performer had to go on without it. In the end, I risked falling down the stairs and injuring myself for nothing. I know people that have gotten seriously injured performing backstage operations. Accidents happen, but doing everything within your power to work safely is your responsibility, both for yourself and for those around you.

I'm not going to mandate an exercise routine for you or make rules about your lifestyle. I will tell you a few things that I wish I had focused on earlier in my career and that I try to incorporate now and plan to continue. Get as strong as you are able to and practice proper form when lifting, whether at the gym or at work. If you need support for your knees, back, ankles, wrists, or any other body part, don't be embarrassed to wear some. If I know I am going to be doing a lot of lifting on a particular day, for example, a load-in or strike, I wear a back brace on my lower back, mostly as a reminder to lift with my legs and not perform any bending and twisting motions (at the command of my chiropractor). If I'm going to be standing for more than six hours, I wear copper knee braces under my pants. If my muscles/nerves in my hand are achy from too much hand-sewing, I wear a brace around my wrist that splints my thumb, so I don't overuse it and cause further injury.

I also focus on flexibility and mobility. Standing for long hours and waiting around backstage followed by intense bursts of activity including heavy lifting, which is what our work can often entail, can wreak havoc on your body. You can be sore, pull a muscle, and get aches and pains all over. Soaking in a hot bath with muscle therapy Epsom salts is a great way to recover after a long day and is great for your muscles. Learning some basic stretches that you can do, even when standing backstage waiting, to keep things loose and limber will help prevent muscle tightness and soreness. If yoga is your thing, I can't recommend it enough. It will help open everything back up that has been constricted during a physically challenging shift. It improves your flexibility and mobility and often focuses on breathwork, which is great for stress relief. If yoga is not your thing, any stretching or flexibility moves you can do will help.

Overall, the physical demand of this job may surprise you at times. Make self-care a priority and focus on performing tasks safely. If you need a second person to lift something with you, don't be afraid to demand it, or find a hand truck, cart, or other assistance. If something is overhead and you are trying to lift it, use proper form and make sure it is not too heavy or awkward before attempting to move it. This can cause a devastating injury if not done properly. Be cautious of the long hours spent standing around on often concrete floors. If anti-fatigue mats can be safely utilized in the places you stand most, request them. Move around, stretch, and take care of your body. Try to get as much sleep as possible, and find ways to ensure continuous, restful sleep as you are able. Stay hydrated, always having water with you in a sealed container so it is easily accessible. The better care you can take of your body, the easier it will be for you to have a long and successful career (and life).

LIGHTS

Anyone who has spent time working backstage can tell you that seeing in the dark can be challenging. Unless you develop night vision, you will want to utilize various lighting elements to help you see what you are doing backstage. Personal lighting instrument options include bite lights, flashlights, neck lights, and head lamps. Additionally, clip lights and other fixtures can be installed backstage to provide light for all crew and cast members to see in dark places.

First, let's discuss personal lights. As you gain more wardrobe experience, you will certainly develop a preference for the type of light you want to use. All the options have pros and cons, but it definitely depends on what works best for you. Personally, I use a bite light secured to a lanyard, worn around my neck. As the name suggests, a bite light is a small flashlight with a flexible plastic case that you put in your mouth and operate with your teeth. Recently, I found bite lights that come in a small leather case, which I actually prefer because it doesn't make noise if you hit it on things and it is easier to operate. You want to have your bite light on a lanyard or necklace of some kind so that when you let it go, it stays attached to you, but you do not have to use your hands for anything involving the light. I prefer bite lights because they are small, allow for easy and hands-free operation, and are inexpensive. The only drawback is that it can make it hard to talk to the performer you are changing (or anyone else) because it is in your mouth. If you need to cue someone to lift their foot or put their arm back, it can be a challenge. This can be helpful though too because often performers are wearing wireless microphones and they can be live (turned on), even if they are offstage, so not talking to them during a change is sometimes for the better. I do not recommend attaching your bite light to elastic of any kind and placing it around your neck, because if it does get caught on something (like a laundry basket) and then becomes uncaught, the elastic can act as a slingshot and the bite light can crash into you, startling you and potentially causing injury or damaging the bite light (you can guess that I discovered this the hard way) (see Figure 5.1).

Figure 5.1 Two styles of bite lights available from Ninja. The top one is attached to a piece of twill tape tied in a knot and the bottom one is attached to a lanyard.

Photograph taken by the author.

Headlamps are flashlights attached to an elastic headband that fits around your forehead (see Figure 5.2). You operate them by pushing a button on the top or side, and they often have various settings. Personally, I don't like headlamps because I think they can be too bright and if I accidentally look toward the stage while wearing one, it can shine onto the stage. I'm also prone to forgetting that it is on, and I find that they give me a headache if I wear them tight enough to stay in place and for the length of an entire show. The advantage is that it is hands-free and leaves your mouth free to verbally cue performers if needed. If you are going to opt for a headlamp, I recommend asking someone from the lighting department for a small piece of blue gel that they can spare. You can cut it to size and tape it over the bulb of the headlamp, which will prevent it from being too bright backstage.

A newer light I learned about recently is a neck light (see Figure 5.3). These are usually two flashlights on the end of a bendable armature that wraps around your neck. You can usually position the lights so they are pointing to different positions, so you could have one aimed up and one down depending on the needs of your quick-changes. They also have dual controls, so you could have only one of the lights on if preferred. I have

Figure 5.2 A selfie of the author taken while running wardrobe wearing a headlamp because a bite light was not feasible when masks were required backstage.
Photograph taken by the author.

heard from a few wardrobe professionals that they now prefer these to other personal light options.

For many years, wardrobe professionals used miniature flashlights. At one point, they even made a bite adaptor that screwed on to the end of miniature flashlights to allow you to safely hold the back of them with your mouth. I recommend keeping a small flashlight in your apron (or otherwise on your person) in case you need to look for something backstage or see in a particularly dark area. For your quick-change lighting solution, I definitely recommend something that is hands-free and easy to turn on and off quickly. You will want to try all of the options to decide what works best for you.

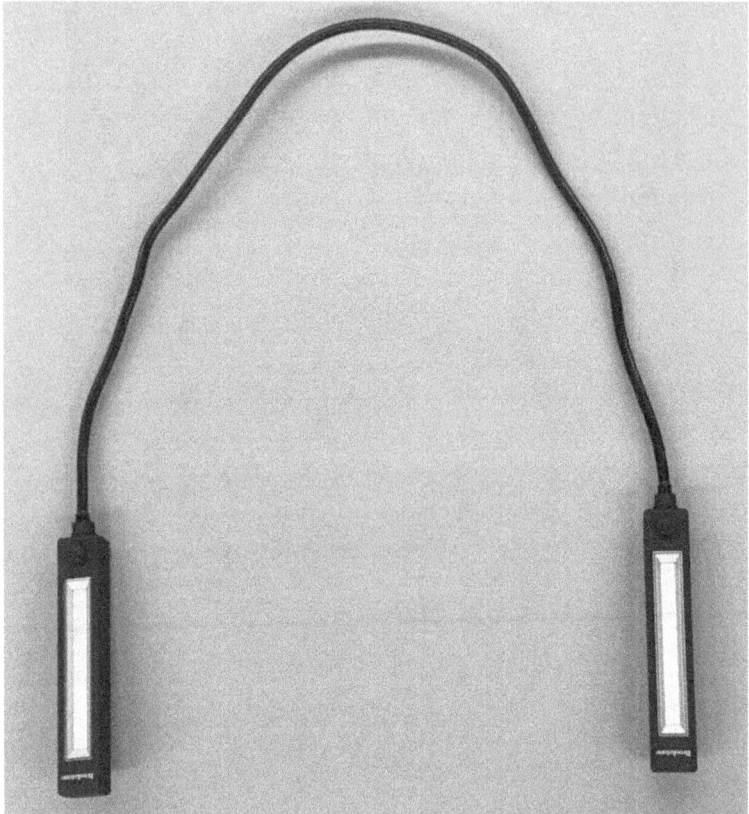

Figure 5.3 A neck light.
Photograph taken by the author.

It is important to be aware of how much light whatever instrument you are using puts out and not to let any light spill out onto the stage where the audience could see it. If you have changes in the wings or close to the stage, try to aim your light towards the backstage area, or do not use your light for these changes. When performing changes in the wings and close to the stage, ambient light from the stage may be enough for you to see. Also, be mindful of shining your light in people's eyes or otherwise distracting or bothering them. The backstage area is dark for a reason, so try not to overuse your personal lighting instruments. You will also want to keep a spare light in your kit or apron so that if your primary personal light burns out or otherwise malfunctions during a show, you will have something to use until you can get your primary light working again. If your light takes batteries or bulbs that can be replaced, always make sure to have spares.

Clip lights, strip lights, and other instruments may be installed backstage to help the cast and crew to see where they are going and what they are doing. It helps to attach a blue lighting gel over the top of the light to soften and darken it and make it less obvious to the audience. This provides enough light but isn't too bright or distracting. I recommend consulting with your technical director and/or production manager for the best lighting options for backstage and the best way to install them. Any cords that need to be run must be taped down, bundled, and secured to ensure you are not creating trip hazards.

Overall, it is important to make sure that the wardrobe crew can see enough backstage to quickly and efficiently check presets, perform changes, and address issues that arise. Combining the use of personal lighting instruments with allowable lighting fixtures backstage can be very effective. Trying out all types of lighting solutions and determining which work best for you is an important part of the wardrobe professional's success. Using personal lighting devices courteously helps you be a good team player.

WARDROBE APRON: WHAT'S IN IT?

Do you remember the scene in *Mary Poppins* where she continues pulling items out of her bag that couldn't possibly have fit in there? Or did your mother ever seem to have the solution for any possible problem stashed in her purse? My wardrobe apron reminds me of this and is a key to my success as a wardrobe supervisor. Let's discuss what items you might want to include in your wardrobe apron and whether or not it has to be an apron at all.

Why is it an apron? I've always imagined it is because waist aprons with large pockets are commercially available, inexpensive, come in black, and are sold at most restaurant supply stores. Aprons are convenient because you tie them around your waist and then it doesn't hurt your back to carry around your supplies. The large pockets allow you to tote around all of the items you could possibly need backstage. It looks nice when you have your backstage black clothing on to have the apron that matches tied around your waist. You can attach things to it and put things in it and they can stay there and be ready for every show, which would not be the case if you tried to put everything in your pants and shirt pockets and then had to wash your clothing. This is what I learned to wear when running wardrobe and what I have seen many wardrobe professionals wear over the years, so it seems to be an industry standard.

I have seen alternatives to the wardrobe apron. Some people wear cargo or tactical pants or jumpsuits with lots of pockets. An amazing draper I worked with developed a pattern for a dresser vest that she had as a beginner sewing project for her students that they then wore to run wardrobe. It had many pockets and even a built-in pin cushion! When the wardrobe crew donned their vests, they looked like an army of some kind headed for battle, it was most impressive. I have seen creative wardrobe people make all kinds of special hip pouches, fanny packs, and apron variations. What matters here is that you find what works best for you and sets you up for success.

Aprons with pockets that are too large can be problematic because it can be hard to find what you are looking for quickly. I like to purchase a waist apron and then sew some lines on the pockets to subdivide them into the sizes I need for my supplies. Attaching a pin cushion or a holder for a nametag to the outside of your apron might be a good idea but try not to attach anything that could get caught on something or someone during a quick-change. Making sure that the ties or waist closure of your apron can be securely fastened and not get caught or cause issues is important. You will constantly be improving your apron as you figure out what works best and what you need.

What is in a wardrobe apron? It depends on the person, the needs of the show, and what supplies are housed backstage. Here is a working list of items to consider (see Figure 5.4):

- Bobby pins, hair pins, wig pins, quick-change wig pins (various sizes and colors)
- Safety pins (various sizes)
- Shoehorn
- Band aids
- Cough drops
- Small mirror
- Sewing kit (thread, needles, needle threader)
- Gaff(er) tape (white and black)
- Mic tape
- Lint roller (miniature)
- Small scissors (with a case so they don't stab you)
- Seam ripper (with a lid so it doesn't stab you)
- Notepad
- Pen
- Permanent marker
- Measuring tape
- Thimble
- Tweezers
- Tissues
- Makeup wipes
- Wet wipes
- Lyol™ wipes
- Hand sanitizer
- Shout™ Stain remover Wipes

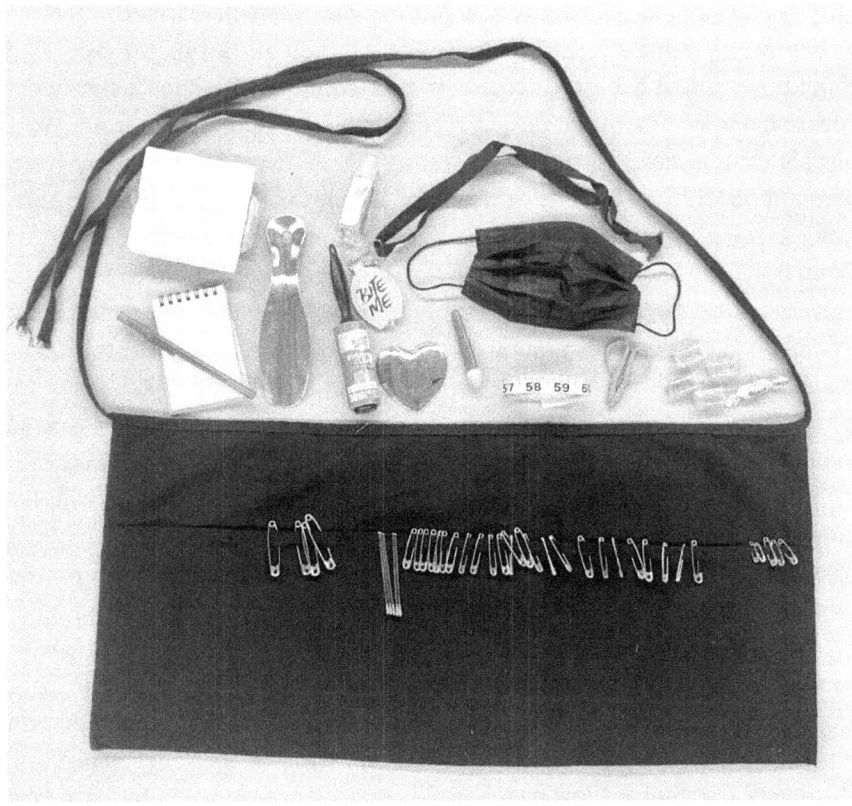

Figure 5.4 The author's wardrobe apron and its contents.
Photograph taken by the author.

- Hairspray
- Superglue
- Double stick tape

This list is by no means comprehensive, and there may be items on here you do not need to have, but it can serve as a starting point. Figuring out what you need and taking notes of things you didn't have but wish you did and then getting them for next time is the best way to cultivate a valuable wardrobe apron. If you choose to use something other than an apron, that's great too. Just make sure whatever you are using can be organized and filled so that you can find things quickly when you need them.

WHAT (AND WHAT NOT) TO WEAR

What should you wear to run wardrobe? Personal style is something that is unique to every individual and chances are you will not be assigned a uniform to wear when running wardrobe. However, some unions or companies may give you a branded t-shirt and ask you to wear it, particularly for load-ins or load-outs from different venues, to identify you as part of the crew who should be granted backstage access. If your company does not dictate what you wear, there are some guidelines I recommend for running wardrobe. Wear black clothing, head to toe. If your shirt or any items have white writing, logos, or decoration, cover it with a piece of black gaff tape or flip your shirt inside-out if the inside is more solid black. I prefer long sleeves to cover my arms, but if the backstage area is too hot and long sleeves could cause you to overheat, short sleeves may be worn, but not tank tops. Try to avoid revealing too much skin, for both practical and professional reasons. Pants, capris, leggings, or shorts are preferable to dresses or skirts because you can more easily move, bend down, crawl on the floor, or do anything else you may need to do. If you prefer a dress or skirt, wear black leggings or tights underneath for modesty and practicality. Clothing should fit well and be practical for moving in. If clothes are too baggy, they may get caught on things or trip you when you are moving quickly backstage. If they are too tight or restrictive, they could prevent you from being able to perform quick-changes and other backstage maneuvers. Some of the more resourceful people I know have constructed or altered their own clothing to wear for running wardrobe. I have seen purchased cargo pants have additional pockets added and padding built into the knees. I have seen jumpsuits constructed that offer pockets of all shapes and sizes. I have seen a large variety of attire worn by wardrobe crew members including overalls, tactical gear, cargo pants, athletic wear, and more. What is important is that you are covered, comfortable, and the fabrics are breathable. There is nothing worse than overheating backstage. It is also good to dress in layers and bring additional items such as a sweater or sweatshirt in case the opposite is true, and it is cold backstage. Be sure that your clothing cannot come undone or get caught on anything or anyone backstage.

Socks and shoes should also be all black. Try to find shoes that have black soles/edges and black laces. If you cannot find suitable shoes, you can tape over colorful logos with black gaff(er) tape and swap out colorful shoelaces for black ones. I prefer sneakers for running wardrobe, because I often find myself running, moving quickly, walking in low-light conditions, and on many different surfaces. They are also more comfortable when I have to stand for ten or more hours a day. Whatever shoes you choose, make sure they are secure (no flip-flops, open toes, or clogs), comfortable, and sturdy. Ensure you can stand in them for a long period of time, or bring a backup pair of shoes to change into if your first pair becomes uncomfortable throughout a long shift. I try to have three or more pairs of wardrobe shoes at a time so that I can alternate them daily throughout the run of a show and even throughout the day if a shift is particularly grueling for my feet.

Try to wear as little personal jewelry as possible. I know this sounds limiting, but it is for practical purposes. If you choose to wear jewelry, be sure it is not large or dangling and has no chance of getting caught on anything. It should also be dark and not reflective. Once, when I was running wardrobe for a concert, I was wearing my wedding ring set (as I had done many times before). On this occasion, I was assisting with load out and pushing a large, heavy gondola down a very long hallway as quickly as possible. Due to obstructions and traffic issues, I was forced too close to the cinderblock wall and my hand was caught between the gondola and the wall. My wedding ring broke my finger, but I was lucky the injury wasn't worse. After that incident, I purchased silicone wedding bands that come in a variety of colors and I wore the black one for all future wardrobe jobs. I completely understand jewelry is a form of self-expression, but it is not worth injuring yourself or someone else while running wardrobe.

Hair should be styled in a way that keeps it out of your face and eyes. If you have long hair and choose to put it up, try not to use large clips that stick out and could get caught on things. If you utilize a headlamp, make sure your chosen hairstyle will allow you to wear the headlamp. Hats may be worn, as long as they are black and low-profile. However you wear your hair, you will want a style that does not need to be touched up throughout the run of the show, choose something that is fix it and forget it and allows you to be comfortable.

Solidifying your personal choices about what to wear to run wardrobe will be an ongoing process. Try different things and reflect after the show about what worked and didn't work about what you wore. If something isn't working for you, don't be afraid to try something new. Ask other wardrobe professionals what they prefer to wear and why. If a particular item works well, I suggest purchasing multiples of it while it is still available. I had a pair of shoes that were amazing for running wardrobe and I wore them for years. When they finally wore out, I was sad to find they were no longer available and wished I had bought a second pair when I realized how comfortable they were. Find clothing items and accessories that express your personality while allowing you to perform wardrobe duties comfortably and safely. Purchase as many options as is practical for your available storage, budget, and lifestyle so that you have different things to choose from for each wardrobe job and shift. Packing a change of clothes to put on after the show ends that is more expressive of your personal style is a great end-of-night ritual. Personally, I love colorful clothing and accessories, so I understand that wearing all black can be a bummer for people. Think of it as a work uniform and bring your clothes with you to the theater and change when you arrive and change back before leaving if it makes you feel better.

IN CASE OF EMERGENCY

Live performance can be a very exciting industry to work in. There is also nothing quite like the moment when something goes wrong in a live performance, and learning to handle the unexpected calmly and effectively is an important part of the wardrobe supervisor's job. Whether it is a costume malfunction, a faulty quick-change, or a missing costume piece, quick problem-solving and decisive action can make a huge difference in the outcome of a problem.

Armed with all the tools in your wardrobe apron, you are ready to act in an unexpected situation. Remember that a temporary fix that can be executed quickly is usually best in these situations. If something rips, try to safety pin it as discretely as possible. If a quick-change is going awry, stay calm and try to focus on each step. If you remain calm, that will help the performer you are interacting with to also be calm, which will help things resolve more easily. If you are struggling with a zipper, getting panicked about it will only cause you to struggle more. Whatever you do, do NOT say anything out loud that alerts the performer to the problem. If you are panicking, the performer will start panicking and everything will go even more off the rails. If a costume piece is missing for a backstage change, assess your options quickly and make a decision. Do you know where the piece is? Is there time to safely retrieve it and get it on the performer before their entrance? If so, you should absolutely do so. If not, what other options do you have? If the performer's next pair of shoes were not set, can they repeat the shoes they were just wearing? This logic is the same for any costume piece. It is the wardrobe team's goal to send the performers onstage in exactly the right costume pieces at the right times. If for some reason on a given day that is not possible, we then try to send the performer out as close as possible to what they should be wearing but also in something that is safe for what they are going to be doing onstage. It is also important for the performer to be on time for their entrance, so you will need to be decisive and efficient. Thinking about solutions and plans of action for potential problems is an important part of wardrobe work so that in an emergency situation you will feel prepared and confident. This is also why it is important to double check all your presets and examine the condition of costume pieces during laundry and preshow prep work, so that missing pieces can be found before they are needed and small repairs can be performed before they become a larger issue during a performance.

When dealing with a malfunctioning costume piece, try to employ a temporary solution that will do minimal damage to the garment and allow for proper fix to be performed later. Gaffer's tape in white and black can be used to reattach trim or accessories or hold a shoe together that has come unglued. Super glue can be a lifesaver for jewelry and other small accessories. If you have time, running a few large hand stitches to hold something together will make it sturdier and you will not risk the holes that safety pins can create in the fabric if placed under tension. Again, trying to plan solutions for potential problems and ensuring that you have the proper tools in your apron for these fixes is an important part of wardrobe work.

The other thing that can happen during live performance is an actual emergency. Whether someone from the cast or crew suffers a medical emergency or the venue itself has an emergency, it is important to prepare yourself for the unexpected. It is a good idea to familiarize yourself with all exits (emergency and otherwise) from all the backstage areas and the location of emergency items such as first aid kits, fire extinguishers and/or hoses, fire alarms, AEDs, eyewash stations, and more. Find out from your supervisor what the emergency procedures and guidelines are and what is expected of you as the wardrobe supervisor in an emergency. If you or someone on your crew is injured, you will want to know who to contact, where to seek treatment, and what procedures need to be followed and what paperwork needs to be filled out to properly report an accident or injury. Talk with the stage management team, production managers, and other backstage personnel to clarify the chain of command for emergencies. During the emergency is not the time to figure these things out or try to find information. Reacting quickly in emergencies can make a big difference, sometimes even between life and death.

This book does not serve as comprehensive training for emergencies, but I can offer you my personal recommendations so that you can be as prepared as possible for the unexpected. Participate in First Aid/CPR (cardiopulmonary resuscitation) training if possible. This is often offered through the Red Cross, but many employers and educational institutions offer it as well. Training for proper use of fire extinguishers and assisting with evacuations is also good training to seek out. Again, many employers offer this, and I would urge you to take advantage of such offerings. Additional trainings to consider include stop the bleed, active shooter, and back safety. My feeling is that you can never be too prepared or have too much information about what to do in an emergency. If you can receive any of the trainings listed or any additional trainings that might be useful to you, definitely do so.

HOW TO SET UP BACKSTAGE CHANGING AREAS

Backstage set-ups will be different for every venue and type of performance you supervise. Having a variety of options for quick-change and backstage changing areas will be useful to you throughout your career. Different types of setups include chairs, baskets, hooks, quick-change booths, and gondolas. Each type has pros and cons and can be useful for different situations. When deciding how to set up a changing area, you will first need to consider what

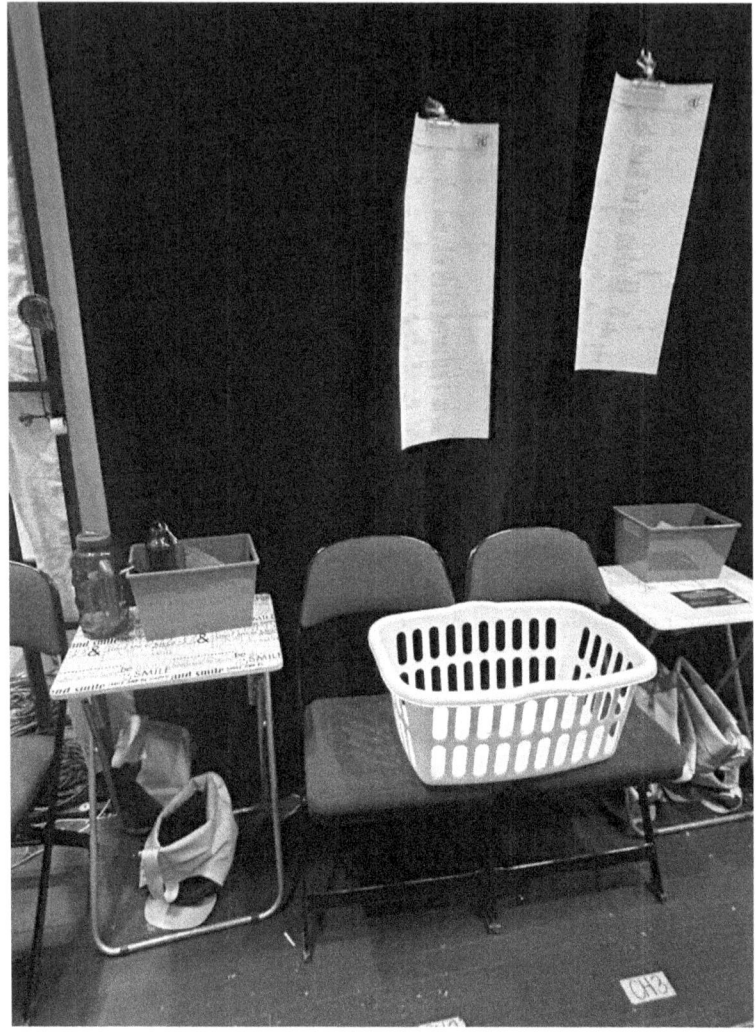

Figure 5.5 Backstage chair, table, and bin quick-change set up in a crossover at The Phoenix Theatre Company.

Photograph taken by the author.

space is available to you backstage and what other things or people need to occupy that space. Coordinating the needs of the wardrobe department with the needs of everyone that utilizes space backstage is important so that people can maneuver backstage effectively and safely. Let's discuss each wardrobe set-up option and how it might be used.

1. Chairs

    Chairs are often used to set up backstage quick-changes. They are a great option because venues usually have extra chairs available. Costume pieces can be arranged on the back of the chair in the order they will be put on the performer. If the seat can be left clear, the performer can sit to put on socks, shoes, pants, and other items that are hard to put on when standing. Accessories can be placed on the seat, in a small basket or box under the chair, or on hooks above the chair if the chair is against a wall. Preset items on chairs turned right side out and opened (unzipped, unbuttoned, unhooked, etc.). No preset items should be on hangers! (see Figure 5.5)

2. Baskets

   Laundry baskets or other small baskets can be used to lay out costume pieces in the order they will be put on the performer. This means that the last item they will put on goes on the bottom of the basket and you stack items from last item to first item they put on and this item is on the top

Figure 5.6 Quick-change baskets loaded before a performance at The Phoenix Theatre Company.
Photograph taken by the author.

of the pile. Empty baskets can also be placed at quick-change stations to catch the items a performer will be discarding during a quick-change to keep items off of the floor and contained for easy clean-up and transport. If you do not have room backstage for a particular quick-change that has multiple costume pieces, they can be placed in a basket that you will bring to the side of the wing or wherever the change will take place. The basket can then double as a discard basket and be quickly removed when the change is completed. Figure 5.6 depicts a large shelving unit with many laundry baskets loaded with quick-change presets backstage at The Phoenix Theatre Company.

3. Hooks

   Often times space is at a premium backstage. Making use of vertical space can help maximize storage options and keep costume pieces off of the floor where they could be trampled, trip someone, or get lost. Hooks on the wall can be a great option for accessories like hats or small costume pieces such as jackets. You want to hang the hooks at a height where they can easily be reached and stagger them enough so that pieces are not hitting each other and getting knocked off. I love to use the sticky hooks that are available in the picture hanging section of the hardware store because they can easily attach to most surfaces and be removed

Figure 5.7 Adhesive hooks mounted to the backstage wall with hats hanging on them at Albright College.
Photograph taken by the author.

without causing damage to walls. The hooks can then be reused with a new adhesive strip (see Figure 5.7).

4. Quick-Change Booths

Another consideration with backstage changes is masking. Depending on what a performer's undergarments are and how modest they are, you should consider backstage changing areas with some type of masking. The most common form of masking is pipe and drape (see Figure 5.8), which can be used to create changing areas. If a large enough area is available backstage, you can create a quick-change booth, which can have multiple stations in a curtained-off area. Stations may include chairs,

Figure 5.8 A changing area set up with pipe-and-drape curtains at The Phoenix Theatre Company.
Photograph taken by author.

baskets, small tables, rolling racks, wig stands, and hanging organizers. Entrances to the booth should be marked with taped-on arrows to indicate where the break in the curtains is located.

5. Gondolas

   The most common type of quick-change set-up for tours is wardrobe gondolas (see Figure 5.9). These are large, rolling cases that have two sides that swing open or a fabric panel that hangs down to be placed backstage and swing shut or latch together for transportation. Some gondolas have lighting instruments in them that can be plugged in backstage to help you see what is inside of them. Many of them have full-length mirrors that

Figure 5.9 Gondola containing costumes from *My Fair Lady* produced by Crossroads Live North America. Costumes designed by Catherine Zuber.
Photograph taken by Coree Howard.

Figure 5.10 Closed gondolas at Crossroads Live North America.
Photograph taken by Coree Howard.

hang on the doors. Gondolas have clothes hanging bars inside of them and can be packed with the costumes for multiple performers divided by rack tags for each performer. Accessories can be stored in hanging organizers (sometimes called ditty bags or accessory bags). Shoes can be stored in the hanging bags or at the bottom of the gondola. Gondolas are incredibly efficient for the load-in and load-out of a tour, because the cases can simply be closed and rolled onto the trucks (see Figure 5.10).

Figuring out what quick-change set-ups work best for each venue and type of performance is an important part of the wardrobe supervisor's job. In addition to lighting, you will want to consider mirrors for your quick-change areas. Full-length mirrors are best because they allow the performers to see all of themselves to double-check that they have things on properly, but even a small mirror that allows them to check their hair and makeup can be helpful.

Cheap full-length mirrors with plastic frames can be taped to walls. Over-the-door full-length mirrors can be attached to the sides of gondolas or other spaces backstage for easy installation. Mirrors are important because if the performers can check themselves and adjust their costumes, it will cut down on some of the work of the wardrobe crew to make sure everyone looks their best before going onstage.

Remaining flexible with your wardrobe set-ups and adjusting things as needed will contribute to your success as a wardrobe supervisor. If you see something while working wardrobe somewhere that is particularly creative or useful, try to take a picture of it so you will remember it for future jobs. Trying different quick-change set-ups and techniques and evaluating them for usefulness and efficiency will enhance your options moving forward. However, try not to change things during the run of a show, as consistency is key. Only change something during a show if a quick-change is not working and needs to be changed.

CHAPTER 6

Tech Week

WHAT IS "TECH"?

"Tech" or "technical" rehearsals are those that lead up to the opening of a production. These include dress rehearsals, but not all tech rehearsals are dress rehearsals. In many theaters, this process is a weeklong, which is why it is often referred to as "tech week". For some productions, the process can be longer, even as long as several weeks. It is important to clarify with the stage management and production management teams which technical rehearsals will be dress rehearsals, and which (if any) will not be. This will allow the wardrobe team time to ensure that costumes are ready when they are needed but also utilize time when the costumes are not being used to perform maintenance and repairs.

The tech process is when all of the technical elements are incorporated into the production. This includes scenery and scenic shifts, props, lighting, sound, special effects, costumes, hair, and makeup. Different technical rehearsals that you may see on the production calendar include the following:

Dry Tech: The stage manager, director, and lighting designer meet to go through the script and identify where lighting cues will happen and the stage manager records preliminary cues in their promptbook.

Cue-to-Cue: Rehearsal utilizing actors and going through the show, skipping to the moment when technical elements change such as scenery or lighting (cutting out all of the dialogue in between).

Tech Rehearsal: The rehearsals that incorporate the technical elements into the show. The show is worked through from beginning to end, stopping and starting as needed for technical areas. Actors are utilized for tech rehearsals. Costumes, hair, and makeup may or may not be used.

Dress Rehearsal: A full run-through of the show in real time utilizing all technical elements, including costumes, hair, and makeup.

Sitzprobe: For musicals or operas, the first chance for the cast to work with the orchestra. May not be in the theater, the cast sings through all of the music with the orchestra.

Quick-Change Rehearsal: A chance for the wardrobe and hair and makeup crew to rehearse extremely fast or complicated quick-changes prior to dress rehearsal. An Assistant Stage Manager (ASM) may be present to assist with a stopwatch and give information on entrances and exits. Crew members and actor(s) will choreograph the specific steps of the quick-change in order to increase efficiency and ensure the change will be as smooth as possible.

Costume Parade: When the director sees all of the costumes for each scene together on the actors, but without any additional design context such as scenery and lighting. Professionally, I have rarely seen these utilized, and as a Costume Designer and Costume Shop Manager, I prefer not to have them.

These represent the most common types of technical rehearsals you may encounter. Every company you work for will have its own tech schedule and types of rehearsals. This is why it is important to ensure that you understand when costumes will be needed and when they will not.

HOURS AND EXPECTATIONS

Actor's Equity Association rules allow for a particular number of **10 out of 12** technical rehearsals. This means that the actors and stage managers can rehearse for no more than 10 hours in a 12-hour period, and a 2-hour break must be provided. For example, the rehearsal could begin at 11:00 am and go until 4:00 pm, have a break from 4:00 pm to 6:00 pm and return from 6:00 pm to 11:00 pm. Crew members are usually called to report to the theater prior to the actors' arrival and stay after the actors leave to do laundry and prepare for the next day's rehearsal, meaning these 12-hour days can be even longer for the crew. As the Wardrobe Supervisor, trying to plan ahead and maximize efficiency can help to keep the hours as reasonable as possible. For example, if you have six wardrobe crew members, can three of them stay later to do laundry and prepare things for the next day and the other three can leave earlier? That way, the three that left earlier can come in early the next day to set up and the three that stayed late can arrive later in the morning, closer to the planned start of the rehearsal. Trying to find ways of balancing the long hours and still getting all of the work that needs to be done accomplished will keep your crew happier during what can be an arduous and stressful process. Tech is full of long hours and short tempers, as everyone working on the production is trying to perfect everything prior to opening night. Trying to plan and prepare as much as possible and approaching each day with patience and tenacity will contribute to your success as a wardrobe supervisor.

Wardrobe crew members should expect their call times (the time they are to report to the theater to start working) to be earlier than the scheduled time for the rehearsal to start and that their end times will likely extend past the scheduled end time of the rehearsal. The crew should plan to be present for the entire rehearsal and take breaks only when directed to. Bringing water (in a sealable container) and snacks to keep in an area that is not backstage that you can quickly consume during a break will help keep you hydrated and nourished throughout the day. Wardrobe team members should limit their cell phone use, particularly in backstage areas, and be sure the notifications and ringer are silenced. I wear a smartwatch (because who doesn't like to see the 20,000 steps they get during a 12-hour tech day), but I set it to "theater mode" and on silent so it doesn't light up unexpectedly during quick-changes. There can be a lot of downtime and waiting around, particularly if costumes are utilized during the tech rehearsals. Bringing a book or computer or phone to occupy the downtime may be acceptable but confirm this with your supervisor and do not let it distract you or cause you to miss something you need to be doing. Wardrobe crew should not leave the backstage area without informing the Wardrobe Supervisor (even if it is just to go to the bathroom) and the Wardrobe Supervisor should inform the assistant stage manager or deck crew chief if they need to step away for any reason. Although it can seem lengthy, tech rehearsal time is very valuable for the designers, technicians, director, and performers, and if a single second is spent looking for a crew member who has wandered away, it can be a huge waste of everyone's time and the company's money.

The wardrobe team should confirm with the stage management and/or production management teams any additional expectations for crew during tech and dress rehearsals. What date should you start wearing all black clothing? Who is required to be on headset and what parameters, requirements, and etiquette are expected regarding that? A general rule is to be as quiet backstage as possible, because you would be surprised how easily the audience can hear backstage noises. I generally forbid wire hangers backstage, because they can be very loud sliding back and forth on a rack and if they fall on the floor or crash against something. I prefer plastic hangers for backstage use. Sometimes you may need to wrap the hanging bar of a rolling rack with tape to prevent the noise of hangers sliding back and forth. This doesn't only pertain to backstage, but sometimes to dressing rooms as well, depending on how close they are to the stage. In one of the theaters I worked at, we had to tape the bars in all three dressing rooms because it was a black box set-up, and the dressing rooms were directly behind the upstage wall. Actors couldn't utilize the bathrooms in the dressing rooms during the show because the sound of a toilet flushing or sink running could be heard by the audience. Some companies will completely forbid cell phone/technology use in backstage areas. A university theater I worked at would collect everyone's cell phone prior to the show and keep them in a locked box in the technical director's office (which was also locked) and then return them after the show (this policy applied to cast and crew alike). Although most companies do not do this, using your technology responsibly and being aware of backstage etiquette and behavior is essential for all crew members.

ATTENDING A RUN-THROUGH

For many live performances, you will be invited to a run-through prior to the start of tech week. This can be called a designer run, a crew watch, or something else. Whatever it is called, it is an important opportunity for the wardrobe team to see the show from the audience's perspective and get a feel for the flow of the production. For musicals or dance shows, you will hear the songs and begin to recognize what is happening when. The more familiar you can be with the show, the better. This will help when you are backstage and need to do tasks in the correct order. If you are invited to multiple run-throughs and are available, I recommend attending all of them.

At the run-through, the wardrobe team is also trying to get a sense of the costume changes. When are they, where are they, and how long are they? As discussed in Chapter 2 of this book, requesting an entrance/exit plot from stage management can be extraordinarily helpful for the wardrobe team to record entrance and exit times. If this paperwork is not available to you, it will be important to devise a system to record entrances and exits. If the production has a script, request a copy of it in advance of the run-through. Work through it and make a chart in the margins for each character's entrances and exits. This way, when you are watching the run-through, you can record the times and locations easily. At the beginning of the run-through, when the stage manager calls "actors go" or "lights up", you will start a stopwatch (either on your cell phone or a separate device). You will keep the stopwatch running throughout the entire first act, only pausing it if a "hold" is called and then restarting it upon the "go" call. These are the times you will record for entrances and exits. Record the entrance time as the second the actor steps onto the stage, even if they are still traveling to their spot. Record the exit time as the time they make it all the way offstage, not when they start heading there from center stage. Remember that these times will be used to calculate quick-change durations, so try to be as accurate as possible.

The locations of entrances and exits are important because it allows you to create a preliminary preset list and track for each side of the stage and for each wardrobe crew member. It will also tell you if a costume piece must be "tracked" during the show, meaning that it will be taken off on one side of the stage and put back on from the other side, so a wardrobe crew member will need to transport the piece to the other side. If your venue does not have a backstage crossover, meaning a way to get from stage left to stage right without being seen by the audience, tracking becomes impossible. If this is the case and you discover tracking issues with costumes at the run-through, it is important to discuss these with the costume designer and potentially the director as some entrances and/or exits may need to be changed.

Location is also important so that you can account for travel time when planning your quick-changes. If a performer exits from one side of the stage and enters from the other, you will want to know how long it takes to get from one side to the other and deduct that from your total costume change time. Sometimes performers enter or exit from unusual locations such as trap doors under the stage, the back of the house (where the audience sits), or from on top of a set piece that takes time to climb up. Accounting for these locations and the travel time needed to get to them is an important part of wardrobe planning. If you are unsure how entrances and exits are being represented in the rehearsal room, be sure to ask questions before the start of the run-through so that you can acquire the most accurate information possible. Once you have timed the show, you can use this information to check changes and create preliminary paperwork prior to dress rehearsals. Referencing the information recorded at the run-through and the actor piece lists, you can determine when a performer is changing. You can then look at the exit time you wrote down prior to their costume change and the entrance time you recorded that will be after their costume change. Calculate the time in between, meaning the time the performer is offstage. This is the length of time for the quick-change. If it is under 5 minutes (or potentially even a little longer if the costumes are complicated or the dressing rooms are far away), you should consider this a backstage change and add the items to your preset lists. If it is under 3 minutes, you will want to assign a crew person to assist with the backstage change, or if the performer will need help getting in and/or out of their costumes regardless of the time allotted. If the change is 2 minutes or less, you may want to assign multiple crew members to assist, depending on the complexity and number of costume pieces involved. When assigning quick-changes to crew members, remember to identify where the changes are taking place and if any travel is occurring. Chapter 3 of this book discusses the creation of wardrobe paperwork, including tracks.

Here is an example of how this works:

Actor/Character	Pg	Line	NT Loc	XT Loc	NT Time	XT Time	Time to Change	Notes
Act 5								
Scene 4								
Actor 6/ Ganymede	49	26		SL		54:34		
Actor 6/ Rosalind	50	110	CENTER		59:59		5:25	In Wedding Clothes

One of the more difficult quick-changes in *As You Like It* takes place in Act 5, Scene 4. During this, the actress playing Rosalind changes from her Ganymede disguise into Rosalind's wedding costume. At the designer run, I was able to record the exit (XT) time and entrance (NT) time and the stage management team had given me this chart, including the entrance and exit locations. In this chart, the NT Loc cell is grayed out if the row is for tracking an exit and the XT Loc cell is grayed out if the row is for tracking an entrance. The NT Time and XT Time cells could also be grayed out for rows where they are not needed, to make it even easier to record times quickly. The wardrobe supervisor was able to determine that there would be 5 minutes and 25 seconds for the change and that it would take place backstage left.

Recording information and timings at the run-through as accurately as possible will help you create a rough draft of your wardrobe paperwork, which is extraordinarily helpful. Chapter 3 of this book discusses the creation of wardrobe paperwork, including tracks.

COSTUME LOAD-IN

Prior to the first dress rehearsal, or the first tech rehearsal if costumes are being used during tech, the wardrobe team will load-in the costume pieces and accessories into the dressing rooms. The more organized and thorough this process can be, the smoother things will be as costumes are incorporated into the production. This is a good time to utilize costume check-in sheets to ensure that the wardrobe supervisor and crew are familiar with the costume pieces and accessories and that all of the needed elements can be located. If any questions arise during the load-in process, it is best to check in with the costume designer and costume staff about pieces that are still under construction or missing items. As you proceed with load-in, make careful notes about any costume pieces or accessories that have been added, changed, or cut (removed). Be sure to communicate any of these changes to your entire crew, as they may affect their individual tracks and many other pieces of wardrobe paperwork.

During the load-in, all costume pieces and accessories will move from the costume shop or wherever they were created or stored to the dressing rooms of the performance space. Easier instances of this include costume shops and theater spaces that are located in the same building or at least the same campus. More complicated instances include costume shops that are across town from the performance space, so everything needs to be loaded onto trucks for transport. If you are moving things to a venue that is not near the costume shop, be sure to pack up a wardrobe box to take with you, which you can request the costume staff's help in creating. This would include spare fabric for built costumes to use for patching or repairs, specialty thread colors that match the costumes, notions (buttons, trim, fasteners, embellishments), touch-up paint for shoes or other painted items, and any additional items that would not be found in a basic sewing/wardrobe kit. You will want to have this box with you at the performance venue for repairs and touch-ups throughout the run of the show.

While loading in, your crew should check off each piece as they hang it on the rack in the dressing room, or place it in a hanging organizer, on a shelf, or on the floor under the rack (as I often do with shoes). This ensures that your crew can identify all of the pieces and that all pieces and accessories are present and accounted for. If you have assigned specific crew members to specific performers as part of their tracks, it is best to have them perform the load-in/check-in duties for their assigned performers. Even though this might take a bit more time, it helps the crew members to get familiar with the pieces they will be working with. During load-in, ask the crew to double-check the items as they handle them. If they find safety pins, stray threads, lint, or other problems, they should address them as they are able or inquire about them with the wardrobe supervisor or the costume staff. Sometimes safety pins are allowed to be used for dress rehearsals and the costume staff is aware, but sometimes an alteration is accidentally forgotten. This is also a good time to make sure all pieces are labeled with the performer's first initial and last name. It is helpful to have spare garment labels, a laundry marker, and small brass safety pins or a micro-tagging gun on hand to add labels during the load-in as needed.

Labeling the performers' individual stations in the dressing rooms can sometimes be the responsibility of the wardrobe crew. Printed sheets with performer names that can be printed with three or four on a page and then cut into separate strips and mounted to mirrors with clear tape is a nice touch. Also, posting the names of all performers assigned to each dressing room on the door is helpful for crew and performers. Making sure the dressing rooms are clean before loading costume pieces in should not be the responsibility of the wardrobe crew, but having glass cleaner, all-purpose cleaner, paper towels, rags, and knowing where the vacuum or broom are located can help expedite the load-in if you arrive and things have not been properly cleaned.

If it has not already happened, load-in may also be the time for you to set up your backstage quick-change areas and any other wardrobe locations at the theater including a quick-change booth if you are using one. Quick-change set-ups are discussed at length in Chapter 5 of this book and prior to this point you should have determined what set-ups you will be utilizing. Bringing all necessary items to the backstage area during the load-in, including chairs, hooks, mirrors, baskets, hanging organizers, clip lights, wig stands, folding tables, racks, shelves, and more and setting up these areas will make the first dress rehearsal run much more smoothly. Figure 6.1 depicts a quick-change preset on a chair. Again, if you have any questions about what can go where backstage or running electrical cords or mounting things, check in with the stage management team, production management, electrics, and scenic personnel. Be sure not to create trip hazards or block anything when setting up your backstage areas.

Taking the time necessary to ensure that the load-in process is thorough, questions are answered, paperwork is updated, and solutions are formulated for any problems that arise will save you and your crew valuable time during the long, stressful days ahead. If items are missing, take the time now to locate them or check-in with the costume staff to determine the whereabouts of the items. Also, if the wardrobe team has any questions about how or when items are worn, now is a good time to reference the fitting photos or consult with the costume designer and costume staff to figure out these details. Being as prepared as possible for dress rehearsals will greatly contribute to your success.

DRESS REHEARSALS

Being as prepared as possible for the start of dress rehearsals is a must for the wardrobe team. As these rehearsals begin, be sure to bring a positive attitude and plenty of patience. Know that many things will change throughout the process, and incorporating changes quickly and efficiently is important. Make sure that the costume designer and their team know that changes to the costumes or when items are worn need to be communicated to the wardrobe team (preferably the supervisor, but at least to a member of the wardrobe crew) and not just to the performer. This way, paperwork can be updated to reflect the most current information, and there will not be confusion between the wardrobe crew and the performer. In addition to keeping my notes app open on my cell phone, I like to keep a small notepad and pencil or pen in my wardrobe apron to jot down changes and adjustments so that I can update everything later. Make sure you are clear on how notes that need to be addressed by the costume staff are to be communicated, and double check that any such notes are properly communicated so that they can be addressed as time allows throughout the process.

Wardrobe tracks and running paperwork are always a work in progress during dress rehearsals and are subject to change. As a supervisor, it is important to instruct your crew to write down everything they do throughout the dress rehearsal process in the order they do it. If additional quick-changes get added to their track, or they transport a costume piece, or assist another crew member with a change that is not assigned to them, they need to make a note of that. These additions can then be added to their track with the next paperwork update. This is important for two reasons, one is that it will help them to ensure that they perform all their duties in the correct order for each performance and the other is so that if someone else must step into their track for any reason, all duties are written down.

If you are new to a venue or company, it is important to discuss how the dress rehearsals will run with the stage management team. These rehearsals can run differently everywhere, and understanding expectations from the beginning will help things run more smoothly. Discuss what will happen when you are approaching a quick-change and what to do if the quick-change does not work. If it is possible, my preference is to go back and try the change again so that the crew and performer can get it right. Sometimes, you will realize that something about the costume needs to be changed in order to make the quick-change in time. Buttons may need to be changed to snaps or Velcro™, a necktie may need to be pre-tied and rigged onto a shirt, or elastic laces may need to be added to shoes so they can be slipped on. If such a discovery is made, you should make a note of it and move on because the change will not get any faster until the adjustments are completed. In this case, you should request a rehearsal of that particular change prior to the next dress rehearsal, once the new rigging has been done. This will allow the crew and performer to practice with the adjustments prior to it being in real time.

For dress rehearsals, you will want to confirm with the costume department if any of the costume pieces will be unavailable for any reason. Sometimes a costume cannot be completed for the first dress rehearsal, and you do not want the wardrobe crew to spend time looking for a piece that isn't there. If a stand-in piece can be provided, particularly for a costume that is involved in a quick-change, that is helpful. If not, it will be important for the crew to mime taking off or putting on that piece so that it gets accounted for in the choreography of the quick-change.

QUICK-CHANGES

Quick-changes, which are changes that are less than five minutes and take place backstage, can be a huge part of wardrobe work depending on the type of production. They can be stressful at times for both crew and performer, but they can also provide extraordinary satisfaction when they go smoothly. As with most aspects of wardrobe work, it is important to remain calm during a quick-change, even if something starts to go wrong. Thinking of a quick-change as an extension of the performance that requires its own choreography helps people understand how to approach it.

Sometimes it is possible to set up quick-change rehearsals prior to the start of dress rehearsals. There are varying opinions about this, because they rarely simulate show conditions. As you can imagine, practicing a quick-change in a well-lit room with plenty of space does not necessarily translate perfectly when you are in a dimly lit backstage area with limited square footage. That said, they can be helpful because you can discover quick-rigging needs prior to the start of dress rehearsals and plan the choreography of the change.

What does choreography mean? When dancers learn steps, they practice them over and over in order until they can execute them perfectly. The same approach can be applied to quick-changes. Both the performer and the crew member(s) need to do the same movements in the same order every time so that the change can run smoothly and be completed in time. It might go something like this:

1. The performer removes their shirt and pants and tosses them into an empty basket.
2. The crew member holds a new shirt so that the performer can easily slip it on.
3. While the performer closes the shirt, the crew member prepares pants so that the performer can easily step into them.
4. While the performer pulls up their pants and closes them while tucking in the shirt, the crew member drops down to help them put on a new pair of shoes.
5. The crew member hands the actor accessories, such as a hat, which they put on.
6. When the change is completed, the performer has time for a sip of water, a wipe with a face towel, and a quick check in a mirror.

This may sound simple, but depending on how much time is allotted for this change or if multiple performers are changing at the same time and a crew member is helping multiple people, the choreography of the change can be very important. If the performer puts a different arm back to slip on the shirt, the crew member may fumble with the change. When the crew member drops down to help with shoes, the performer should always lift the same leg first. If they change what they have done, the crew member may not have the correct shoe going on the correct foot. Personally, I have been hit in the eye socket with a performer's knee during a quick-change because the performer moved in a way they had not moved before. Defining the steps of a quick-change as specifically as possible and practicing them so that the performer and crew member both feel comfortable and confident is essential to successful quick-changes.

Another key to success is how items are preset. Do not preset items on hangers! If an item is on a hanger, remove it from the hanger prior to the change. Open all closures (or at least those that need to be opened for the performer to put on the costume piece). If you are setting items on a chair or in a basket, make sure you set them in the reverse order that they need to be put on, so the last item they will put on is at the bottom of the pile and the first item is on top. Double check that sleeves are turned right side out, pant legs are fully extended, and which side of the garment is the front and which is the back. There are some elements of presets that are open to personal preference. Wardrobe crew members should discuss with the performers what will work best. Pooling a skirt on the floor so that the performer can step into it and then pull up the waistband might work well for one person, while holding the skirt open and handing the performer the waistband so they can step into it, and you can fasten it, might work better for someone else. Be careful when placing costume pieces on the floor. You never know how clean the backstage area is and you do not want to risk staining or damaging the costume piece. If pieces are preset on the floor, you may want to use a drop cloth or towel underneath that can be removed after the change.

If a change is not running smoothly, there are various solutions you can try. Changing how something is preset to make it faster to put on might help.

Figure 6.1 Costumes preset on a chair backstage at Albright College.
Photograph taken by John Pankratz, Ph.D.

Can anything that is being put on in the change be worn under the previous costume or can any of the pieces being removed stay on under the new costume? The process of wearing some elements of the performer's next costume underneath their current costume is called underdressing, and it can cut down tremendously on the time needed for a change. Underdressing only works if the extra pieces cannot be seen underneath the first costume and do not cause fit issues or other unwanted problems. Also consider the order a change is choreographed in. Would it be faster if one step came before another step instead of after? Could the crew member be helping the performer more if one step was swapped with another? Sometimes crew members are timid about taking control of the change and helping the performer with closures, tying shoes, or placing accessories. If there is time for the performer to do things themselves, that is fine, but in a fast quick-change, it is important for the crew member to help as much as possible.

Practicing quick-changes on your own can help you feel more confident when you are doing them with the performer. Putting the costumes on and taking them off of a dress form can help you get faster at the closures. If you do not have a form available, you can do the same thing with a hanger. Familiarize yourself with the costume pieces so that you can easily tell the front from the back, the inside from the outside, and know what order the pieces go on in and how they should be put on. If you have questions about something, be sure to communicate with the costume designer to confirm how things should look so that you are sending the performers out looking their best.

Quick-changes will probably always give a rush of adrenaline to the crew members and performers. Allowing that to be an advantage rather than a hindrance is an important skill to master. In the moments before a performer runs toward me for a difficult quick-change, I like to walk through the change in my mind, reminding myself of the choreography of the change and picturing myself executing it successfully. Although it can be stressful, the pride I feel after executing a smooth quick-change is one of my favorite parts of the job. If things start to go awry with a quick-change, I try to remain calm and reassure the performer. Panicking will not make anything go faster, so learning to remain cool and collected in the face of the unexpected will contribute to your success as a wardrobe professional.

WIG AND MAKEUP CHANGES

Some quick-changes will incorporate wigs or hair and makeup changes also. Many productions will have crew members specifically assigned to this area who will work alongside the wardrobe crew to execute these changes. In this case, you will want to coordinate with them to choreograph their work with the costume change so all of the steps can be planned in the most efficient order. It is also important to be aware of where they need to stand to access the performer to do their work. Choreographing the change so that all crew members can access what they need to have the change run smoothly is even more important with multiple crew members.

I have worked with Kelly Yurko, an Associate Professor at the University of Cincinnati's College Conservatory of Music and the head of their wig and makeup MFA program, for years and she has taught me valuable skills in this area. I asked her for specific recommendations for wardrobe professionals and she offered the following advice.

1. Rehearse quick-changes in the light first so that everyone can see what is happening and ensure efficiency and performer safety.
2. Choreograph the change including the movements of the performer and all of the crew members.
3. Plan the order of the change for efficiency. Depending on the height of the performer and crew members, putting on a wig may require the actor to sit down. The best order may be for the wig crew person to remove the first wig quickly, then for the costume change to proceed, followed by the performer sitting in a chair and the wig person pinning on the new wig. Once the performer is sitting, the wardrobe crew can continue adding socks, shoes, accessories (jewelry), and other costume elements, but staying out of the way of the wig crew member while doing so. If makeup or facial hair needs to be changed, this can also be done with the performer sitting down if it is easier.
4. Don't forget to involve sound! If the performer is wearing a wireless microphone and pack, it could be located in their wig prep. At the very least, have the sound person standing by when you rehearse the change to ensure you do not pull something out of place and that nothing goes wrong with the microphone. (This is a great note for costume quick-changes also, because performers may be wearing the pack on their body with a pack and belt.)
5. Inform the wig and makeup crew how the costume pieces need to come off and be put on (over the head, dropped to the floor, etc.) to help them plan their movements. Will the performer be bending down?
6. Utilize singular wig stands for wig quick-changes. These are often pieces of PVC pipe that are cemented into a bucket base that a foam or canvas head can be put on to hold the wig in a hands-free manner. Figure 6.2 depicts a wig stand made to sit on top of a table, where the PVC is cemented into a small pot.

You may work on productions where there are not crew members assigned to hair and makeup changes and it becomes part of the wardrobe crew's work. If this is the case, you will want to add additional items to your wardrobe

Figure 6.2 A quick-change setup backstage at The Phoenix Theatre Company utilizing a tabletop wig stand made from PVC pipe cemented into a small bucket.
Photograph taken by Kelly Yurko.

apron to help facilitate hair and makeup. These may include hair pins, bobby pins, double-sided grooming tape, a small hand mirror, makeup wipes, alcohol wipes, hairspray, a comb or brush, and hair elastics. If you are not sure how to remove or pin on a wig, you should consult the wig designer or supervisor for instructions. You can make special "quick-change hairpins" by slightly bending the u-shaped end of a 3" long hairpin, so that it would stick up from the head. Another option is to attach a small pearl/bead to the hairpin at the "u" so that you can more easily find it to pull it out in a quick-change (see Figure 6.3). It is important to know exactly how many hairpins are holding the wig on the performer's head and their exact locations before trying to remove them. You do not want to pull out pins that are holding the style of the wig in place. When pinning on a wig in a quick-change, you can use as few as four pins. They should be placed at the temples on either side and the nape of the neck on either side. Make sure the pins get through the wig lace/base, the wig cap(s), and anchor into the performer's own hair. I like to ask

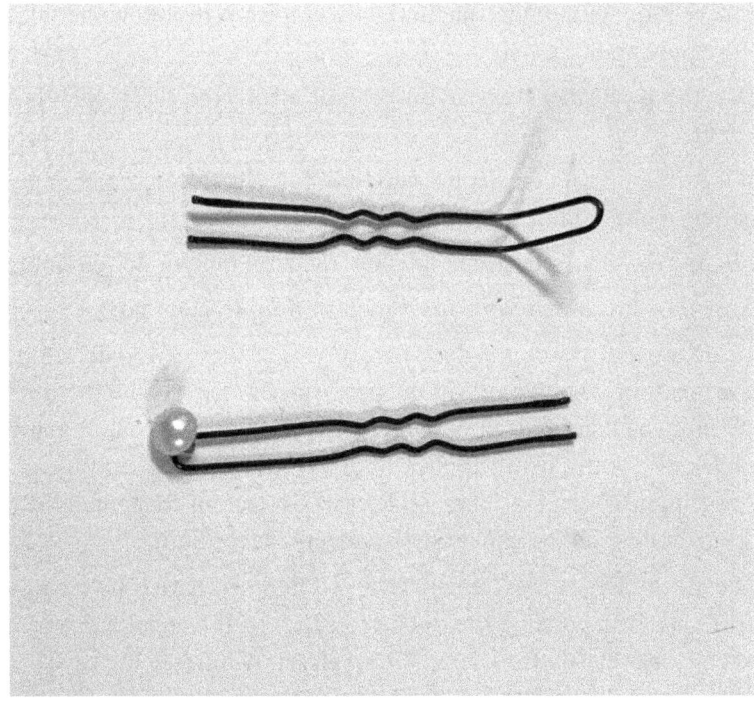

Figure 6.3 Hairpins designed for quick-changes. The top one is bent up at an angle and the bottom one has a pearl attached at the "u".
Photograph taken by the author.

the performer after each pin if it feels solid, because they are able to feel if it is pinned securely. Again, keep track of how many pins you put in and their locations, so it is easier to remove later.

If makeup is part of a quick-change, consult the makeup designer for directions for the makeup application. It may be easiest and quickest for you to hold a mirror up for the performer and hand them items so they can apply the makeup themselves. If this is not possible, you can apply makeup for them, or if two wardrobe crew members can work together, one can be applying makeup while the other is doing the costume change.

Artificial facial hair is an additional item that you may encounter as a wardrobe professional. Sometimes it can be added during a quick-change, so knowing how to properly apply it is an important skill to master. There are two primary techniques for applying facial hair: Using spirit gum to glue it on and sticking it to the face with double-sided grooming tape. Spirit gum is the preferred method because it tends to hold better, move more naturally with the face, and does not shine or reflect through the lace on which the facial hair is mounted. However, if the facial hair needs to be applied and removed, double-sided tape is the easier option for removal. Spirit gum must be removed slowly with spirit gum remover to avoid damage or injury to the performer's face. With either method, you will want to follow the following steps for applying facial hair:

1. Dry the performer's upper lip or face where the facial hair is to be applied.
2. Wipe the area with an alcohol wipe and fan it with your hand or a small, battery-powered fan.
3. Change the wig or costume to allow the area time to dry completely.
4. Apply the facial hair with spirit gum or double-sided tape.

Cutting a paper towel into four pieces so that they can easily fit in your apron is great for drying/blotting the performer's face. With either method, you can prep the facial hair piece, either by applying a thin coat of spirit gum to the back of it with a brush applicator or by sticking one side of the double-sided tape to the back of it. Then fold down a corner of the remaining paper so you can easily pull the paper off to apply the facial hair.

If the quick-change is extremely fast, you may not have time for either of these options. It is possible to attach the edges of the facial hair to a piece of stretchy, clear elastic cord (used for jewelry making) (see Figure 6.4). This could go around the performer's head or loop around their ears. This method is best if the facial hair is very large, so the cording wouldn't extend too far

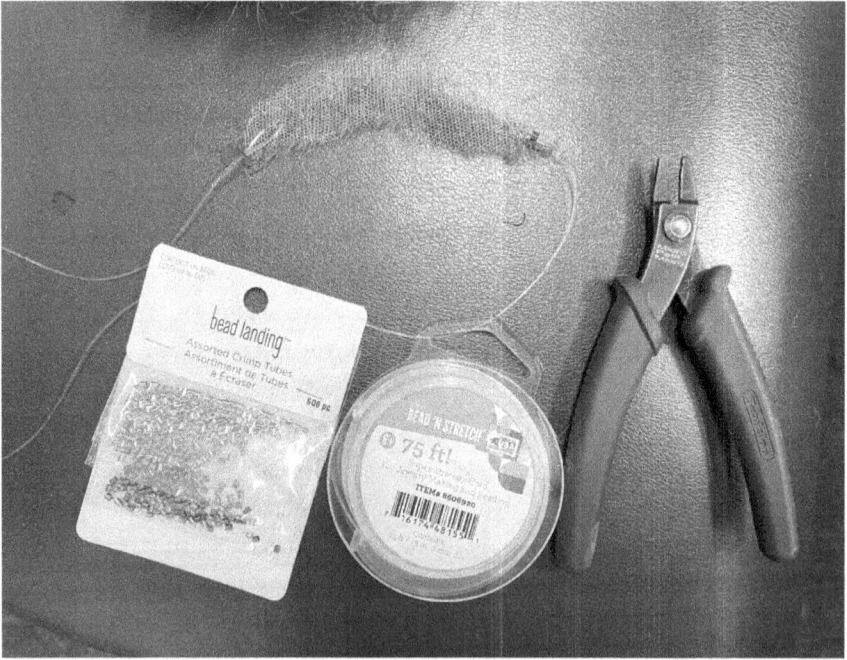

Figure 6.4 An artificial mustache ventilated onto wig lace with clear elastic attached to the sides using a crimp tube, and the pliers used for crimping.

Photograph taken by Kelly Yurko.

across the face or if it does not need to look super realistic. This method can cause an indentation in the performer's cheeks, which can look strange and be uncomfortable, but it is an option.

Familiarizing yourself with basic wig, hair, and makeup skills will be a great help to your work as a wardrobe professional. Confirming what aspects of this you are responsible for, if any, is an important step in the process.

DRESSING ROOM ORGANIZATION

Productions can have a seemingly endless amount of costume pieces and accessories. Organizing them effectively and efficiently will help cut down on the panic of missing a costume piece before or during a performance. This organization starts in the dressing rooms. Having a system for performers to easily identify which costume pieces belong to them is essential. Rack tags can hang on clothes hanging racks and be labeled with the performers' names and their character names. Generally, racks are arranged left to right, as if you are reading a book. The rack tag is placed at the far left and the costumes for the performer are to the right of their tag. The next rack tag is then placed, and those performers' costumes are placed to the right of their tag. Hanging organizers (sometimes called ditty bags) are used for accessories and will also be hung with the performer's costumes. Personally, I like to put the hanging organizer at the end of the costumes, just before the next performer's rack tag. This way, the costumes are "book-ended", and it is easy to know whose items are whose. Also, if the rack tag shifts a little bit, the hanging organizer can be a good indicator of the end of one performer's pieces and the beginning of another. This is not everyone's preference, however, so be sure to clarify how it is going to be done and keep it consistent.

Accessory storage can be problematic in some dressing rooms. There seems to be an endless number of hats, shoes, jewelry, and other accessories that need storage. Hanging racks in dressing rooms with shelves on top of them are ideal because accessories can be placed on the shelves. Shoes can easily be stored on the floor below the performer's costumes or in large pockets on the hanging organizer. Figure 6.5 depicts shoes stored on a small shoe rack below hanging costumes and accessories stored on a shelf above. Figure 6.6 depicts a gondola with a hanging organizer for hats, rack tags to separate the costumes, and laundry baskets below. If more accessory storage is needed, multi-pocket hanging organizers can be attached to the back of the door or hung on the rack and then labeled for each performer. If small accessories (such as jewelry) are being used, sometimes a small plastic bin with a lid or a baggy labeled for the performer and then placed on the dressing room counter is a good solution.

Hangers are an important part of dressing room organization. You should provide a hanger for every costume piece that is appropriate for the garment that is being hung on it. Clip hangers are ideal for pants or skirts to keep

Figure 6.5 Costumes hung in a dressing room with a shoe rack below and an accessory storage rack above at The Phoenix Theatre Company.

them from getting wrinkles from being folded over a hanger after pressing or steaming. Hangers with indentations for hanging loops or thin straps can help keep costume pieces from falling off. Wooden hangers are good for suit coats and outerwear. Having extras of each type of hanger in the dressing room will help ensure everything is hung up at the end of a performance.

Developing a system of dressing room organization that works for you, your crew, and the performers is essential to your success as a wardrobe supervisor. Trying different strategies and adjusting them as you go and being open to trying new things for different spaces and personnel will help things run as smoothly as possible. Knowing that the same system won't work for all venues or productions and having various options will help you adapt as you go through your career.

Figure 6.6 Wardrobe gondola with hanging organizer for accessories, rack tags to separate costumes, and laundry baskets below.

Photo compliments of Crossroads Live North America and taken by Coree Howard. Costumes designed by Catherine Zuber.

PROBLEM-SOLVING

Dress rehearsals during tech week can be chaotic, stressful, and exhausting. Often everyone involved with the production works long hours with few or no days off. Less sleep and more stress can cause tempers to flare and patience to be in short supply. Trying to maintain a positive and collaborative attitude is the best thing you can do in this situation. Providing confident, calm leadership for your crew will help them navigate challenges as they arise. Focusing on communication and problem-solving will help resolve issues quickly.

When attempting to resolve a problem, first determine what the desired outcome is. Then determine what options are available to address the issue. If small accessories are continuously getting lost backstage, alternate storage solutions may be needed. A tiny jewelry box that fits into a wardrobe apron may be a great solution. If a quick-change is taking too long for the allotted time, is it possible for another crew member to help with the change?

Sometimes there are larger problems that arise during technical rehearsals. Maybe you don't have enough crew members to execute a particular change sequence within the given time. It will probably not be possible to hire additional crew members, so you will need to discuss this problem with production management and the director. Is it possible for some of the performers to exit earlier or enter later so that their needs are more staggered, and the crew members can help everyone? Do not be afraid to ask for help with issues that seem larger than what you can handle. However, try to determine potential solutions before bringing up an issue with the production team. By working together, the needs of everyone can be met.

Speaking of meeting needs, self-care is especially important during tech and dress rehearsals. Be sure to take breaks, when possible, for yourself and your crew. Drink water and don't skip meals. Being hydrated and nourished will go a long way for your energy and your mood. Getting enough sleep can be difficult during this time but try your best to establish routines that allow you to get as much sleep as possible. During a 10 out of 12, do you have time for a quick nap during the two-hour break? Personally, I also like to find time for exercise each day, even if it is just a walk around the block on a break. Maybe you like to meditate or stretch. Try to find little ways of practicing self-care during long, stressful workdays and get fresh air if possible. Modeling this behavior for your crew will make you an amazing role model as a wardrobe supervisor.

CHAPTER 7

Performances and Costume Maintenance

REFINING YOUR ROUTINE

After the show opens, it is important to refine your routine to make it sustainable for the entire run of the show. The length of a run varies greatly from production to production. Longer runs allow you plenty of time to refine your routine whereas shorter runs will allow very little time. The more comfortable you get with the show, the easier it is to see where you can make adjustments. Maybe you discover that if you track a costume piece earlier, you won't have to run after a quick-change to track it, or that a costume piece is dead (meaning not worn again in the show) after a certain change so it can be returned to the dressing room or dropped into the laundry basket. You want to adjust things that make your work more efficient and help the show run more smoothly. Otherwise, you want to settle in your track and the show and have everything become a solid routine. It can get monotonous, but repetition and consistency are important for everyone to feel comfortable. Having a solid routine will help you deal with any surprises or issues that arise during a performance. You will know how much time you have to solve something or who else from your crew is available to assist with an issue. This is also a good time to adjust the call time if things have been getting consistently faster. You may have started with the call an hour before half hour (90 minutes to show) and now find that the crew is consistently finished with pre-show tasks well before the half hour call. If this is the case, you may be able to adjust to a half hour before half hour (60 minutes to show), as long as all of the work can get done and the costumes are taken care of. These small adjustments are appreciated because nobody likes to feel like they are wasting time.

This is also a good time to ensure that your paperwork is complete and updated. I believe that one of the hardest parts of the wardrobe supervisor's job is wrangling the notes of the crew. If you or your crew have added to or changed anything about your tracks, you want to make sure the changes are

DOI: 10.4324/9781003425274-8

reflected in the paperwork. Sometimes crew members think small adjustments are no big deal and they don't need to write them down. For example, if a crew member tracks a costume piece from stage left to stage right for another crew member because they are traveling anyway and it saves the other crew member a trip, it might not get recorded. If someone steps in to cover the track of the first crew member and they don't bring the costume with them and the second crew member doesn't double check before the quick-change, the item may be missing when it is needed. This is why it is important to update your paperwork and that of your crew once everyone's tracks are solidified. This also gives you an accurate representation of the run of the show, so if you ever work on the show again, you do not have to start from scratch creating everything.

Another thing that happens during show runs is confusion from show to show. You find yourself thinking things like "did I do this change already?" or "what comes next?" or "where are we?". When you are doing the same show day after day, it is easy to get confused from moment to moment. There are different ways of dealing with this, and having a consistent, solid routine definitely helps. If you know you do this task first, followed by this one, and so on, it is easier to stay on track. You might find it helpful to write up small index cards with prompts for your track. They could just list the changes you assist with in order and their location. You could even type these up and laminate them and put a small checkbox next to each one and cross them off with a dry erase marker as you move through the show. Hanging up show order lists backstage is helpful for all crew and cast members. If you get confused as to where you are in the show on a given day, you can reference the list and figure out what's next. These issues are compounded on double show days, as the sense of Déjà vu can be confusing. Again, being consistent and thorough with your routine and following your track on paper will help make sure that you complete all of your tasks for each performance. Although it may be your 100th or 1000th show, it is likely the audience's first time seeing it and they deserve to see the best performance possible, and it is our job to help provide that.

CONSISTENCY OF THE INTEGRITY OF THE DESIGN

Part of the wardrobe supervisor's job is to keep the costume design consistent and maintain its integrity. As expected, this is easiest to do on shows with short runs and gets progressively harder the longer a show runs for. What does this mean and how do you accomplish it? It means double checking that costumes are in good repair and are being pressed and steamed (as required) prior to each performance. It means confirming that performers continue to wear the costumes correctly and as the costume designer intended them to. It means consulting the list of accessories and ensuring they are all still being worn when and how they are supposed to be. It can mean making small alterations to costumes if performers fluctuate in size throughout the run so that the costumes fit appropriately. It can even mean coordinating for something to be rebuilt or replaced if it gets to a state of disrepair.

Unfortunately, you will be faced with tough situations when it comes to maintaining the costume design. A performer may not like their costume from the beginning but decides to wait until after opening to change how they wear it or even stops wearing it completely. It is the wardrobe supervisor's job to intervene in this situation. You need to discuss the issue with the performer as professionally as possible. Begin by approaching it as an assumed mistake. You can say, "I noticed you wore a different shirt for Act 1 yesterday. Was your other shirt missing or does it need a repair?". This sounds nonaccusatory, and you are offering solutions to a problem. Hopefully the performer will say, "Oh I'm sorry, I forgot I was supposed to wear it" or something similar and the issue will be resolved. However, if this is not how it goes, your end goal is to have the performer wear their costume pieces as the designer intended. If a calm, professional discussion does not reach this goal, you may have to escalate the situation. Start by discussing it with the production stage manager or the assistant stage manager most closely affiliated with wardrobe concerns. If they cannot help you reach a resolution, you may need to involve company management, production management, or others in a higher capacity to assist. The most important thing is finding a solution that preserves the integrity of the original costume design. If you get a reputation as a wardrobe supervisor who does not do this, it will be hard to advance in your career. Now there are situations where performers will change something that doesn't affect the integrity of the design. They might prefer wearing their own bra rather than the one provided. If the look is the same and the bra isn't showing or causing issues, you can allow this. A performer might prefer one dance trunk to another when they were provided with two pairs for under different costumes. If the color of them and the look remain the same, there is no reason to force them to wear both pairs. Deciding when an issue needs to be addressed will require your discretion as to what affects the integrity and consistency of the original costume design.

MAINTAINING THE COSTUMES

A large part of maintaining the integrity of the costume design involves maintaining the actual costume pieces. This encompasses laundry, repairs, starching, pressing and steaming, repainting, small alterations, and more. The more you know about proper costume maintenance, the more successful you will be as a wardrobe supervisor. It is important not to make assumptions about what your crew members know about maintenance and train them how you would like these things to be done. Learning and double-checking equity rules regarding costume maintenance is an important step in ensuring you are executing your job to the best of your ability. Also, you may want to check in about any expectations or standards of each organization you work for.

Let's begin with laundry. This is an extremely important part of taking care of the costumes throughout a run. Actor's Equity Association rules require skin parts (t-shirts, socks, bras, dance trunks/belts, hosiery) to be laundered before every performance. This often requires doubles of these items if there will not be sufficient time between the performances to launder them. If this is going to be the case, it is good to discuss this with the costume staff and designer prior to the beginning of dress rehearsals to ensure that additional items will be provided. A good practice for dealing with skin parts, which can be difficult or cumbersome to label, is to issue each performer a mesh zippered laundry bag. Label the bags with numbers or letters and assign one to each cast member and keep a list of which performer has which letter or number. Instruct them to put small items (socks, bras, dance trunks, mic belts, and hosiery) into the mesh bag and zip it before placing it in the laundry basket (see Figure 7.1). Remind them not to ball up their socks or wad up anything as it will not dry thoroughly and it isn't pleasant for the wardrobe team to have to reach in and unroll someone's sweaty socks, nor for the performer to put on damp items for the next performance. The mesh bag system is a great way to organize small items for each performer and not have to go through the process of labeling socks and then relabeling them for every show. Another great tip I recently heard from Lucinda Koenig at The Phoenix Theatre Company is to purchase small, drawstring muslin washable bags for each performer to use as a wash bag for their mic belt. Because mic belts often have large pieces of Velcro™ on them, they can damage other costume pieces, even if the Velcro™ is closed and they are in a mesh bag. After seeing one too many tights that met their doom by tangling with a mic belt, Lucinda came up with this great solution. She labels the muslin bags with the corresponding letter or number for each performer. She instructs the performer to match the Velcro™ and place the mic belt in the bag and cinch the drawstring and then she washes them. After washing, she hangs them to dry and places the muslin bag on the same drying hook so that they can be placed back inside the bag and returned to the performer for the next performance. Do not have performers put undershirts in mesh or muslin bags, as they will not dry. Instead, label these with the corresponding letter/number for the performer and have them place them loose in the laundry basket.

Aside from skin parts, it is important to launder costume pieces on a regular basis. You will want to create a laundry schedule to ensure that all items are laundered at least weekly. Items that cannot be laundered will need to be sent for dry cleaning weekly. Some items may require special care, such as hand washing, so that should be noted as well. Items may require hang drying, lying flat to dry, or a low-heat dryer setting. It is good to indicate on the laundry schedule how items should be cared for so that the crew doesn't have to stop and read all of the care tags inside the garments every night. Some costumes may need to be laundered more frequently. Even when worn with an undershirt, a dress shirt worn for the entire show or during a vigorous dance number may need to be washed nightly. A costume that is worn for a single scene or by a performer who does not perspire much may only need a weekly washing. It is good to have a laundry schedule created prior to dress rehearsals, but you can edit it as you discover how often each piece needs to be cleaned.

Prior to washing anything, it is important to sort items by color and notice if any of them have stains or other damage. You will also want to check (and double check) the pockets of all of the costume pieces to make sure nobody accidentally left something in there. You will often find props, makeup, cough drops, tissues, and other items that could potentially ruin the load of laundry or the item if washed. If something is ripped, it is better to repair it before washing so it does not fray or get worse. If stage makeup or a consumable item has stained a costume, you will need to pre-treat it with stain remover prior to washing. You do not want to wash and dry the item and risk setting the stain. The best stain remover for almost all stains is SARD™. If you use SARD™, you will want to wipe away any of the stain that you can with cold water and a cloth. You will then apply a layer of SARD™ to the stain (I prefer the stain stick option, but it is also available in a bar, which is slightly cheaper). Then let the stain remover sit on the stain for a little while and then agitate it with a soft bristle brush or a clean cloth. Then launder the item as normal and hopefully the stain will be gone. This product works wonders on stage makeup and fake blood. OxiClean™ is also wonderful and can be mixed with a little water to create a paste and applied to a stain and lightly agitated. The strangest stain removal technique I will offer is for blood. When someone says they got blood on something, I always ask them whose blood it is. They will often look at me strangely, wondering why I would ask this. The reason is that your own saliva will remove your blood. I'm not a scientist, so don't ask me why this works (I have heard something about enzymes), but what I do know is that if you bleed on a garment accidentally and then you rub the blood spot with some of your own saliva, it will come out (and you will then need to wash or otherwise disinfect the garment). If it is not your blood and there is a blood stain, you will want to try hydrogen peroxide to remove it. After stain removal and repairs are performed, you will want to run the wash with cold water and a free and clear detergent. Do not add fabric softener. If you are mixing colors in your load, ensure that none of the items are dyed or have colors that will run and stain the other costumes in the load. If you are unsure, wash the item separately first with a Shout Color Catcher™ and see if it picks up any dye. If it does, you will want to continue to wash the item separately until no dye comes off. To prevent yellowing and keep white clothes bright, mix some OxiClean™ in with the wash load. Do not use bleach for whitening whites unless you can be absolutely sure you clean every drop out of the machine before running another load, as it can ruin colors. Absolutely do not use bleach if you share your machines with the costume shop or anyone else. Here are some common stain types and the best removers for them:

STAIN REMOVERS AND THEIR USES	
Type of Stain	**Stain Remover**
Grease/Oil	Dawn™ Dish Soap
Grease/Oil	Janie Dry Stick Spot Cleaner™
Blood	Hydrogen Peroxide
Dirt/Other	Shout™ Spray
Stage Makeup	SARD™
Yellowing Armpits	Vinegar
Grass, Dirt, Blood, Foods, Grease, Oil, Perspiration, Rust, and Color bleeds	ZOUT™ Spray

When the wash is finished, you will sort the load and place items that can be dried by machine into the dryer. Don't forget to clean the lint trap so that the machine will operate efficiently, and you will reduce the risk of a fire. Use a dryer sheet labeled "free and clear" and the dryer setting appropriate for the costumes. Some people prefer not to use dryer sheets, which is fine. If you don't, I recommend using dryer balls to help reduce static and keep the clothes from clumping together and not drying. Hang up line dry items on a clothes drying rack or clothesline and lay "flat to dry" items on dry towels on flat surfaces. Double check the performers' mesh bags to see if the items inside are hang-dry (such as bras and hosiery) or machine-dryable (such as socks and dance trunks). If they can be machine dried, place them in with the rest of the costumes to be dried (in the bags, zipped up). If they need to be line dried, there is a wonderful system of placing plastic hooks on a rolling rack as pictured in Figure 7.2. Label the hooks with the letters or numbers associated with the bags and hang the corresponding items on the rack. You can run the empty mesh bags zipped up with the dryer load and keep the hang-dry items on the hook until they are dry. When you go to distribute the laundry the next day, you can place the items back in the bags before distributing them.

In between washings, it is important to use wardrobe spray to kill bacteria and reduce odors. The most common industry practice is to put inexpensive vodka into a large spray bottle and label it "wardrobe spray" or "cleaning fluid". If you are worried about someone consuming it, you can cut a dryer

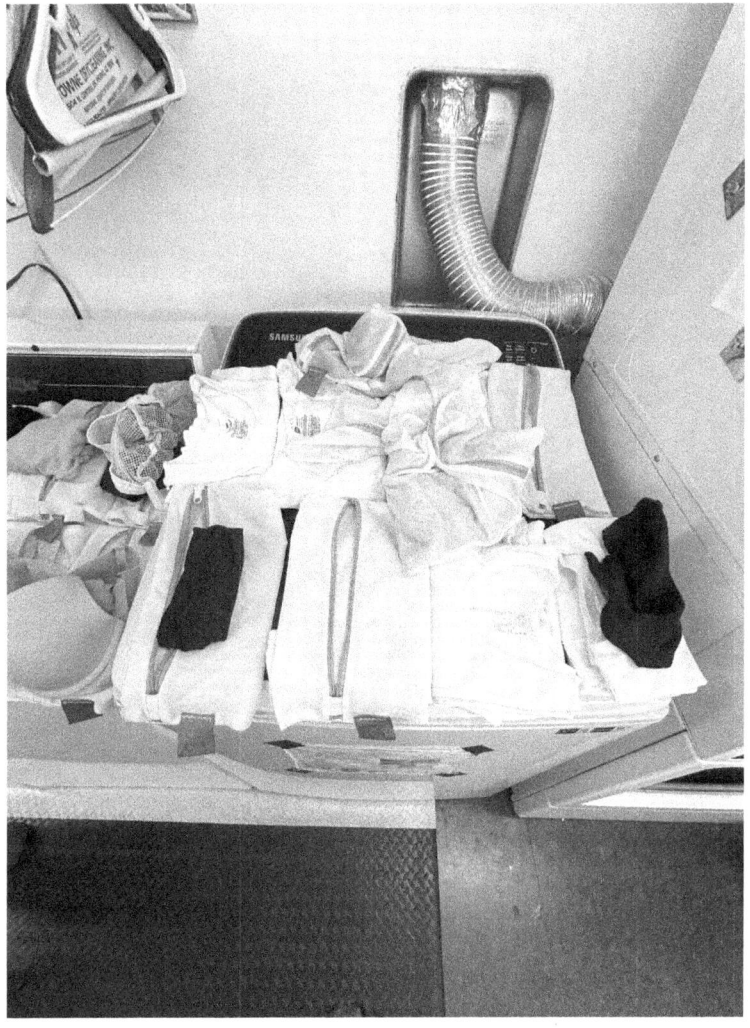

Figure 7.1 Mesh laundry bags with the items placed on top of them being prepared for distribution at The Phoenix Theatre Company.
Photograph taken by the author.

sheet in half and put it in the spray bottle and then fill it with vodka. If you cannot purchase or store alcohol where you are working, some people have suggested high-percentage rubbing alcohol can be used instead, but I have not tried this. Mixing a small amount of essential oil such as tea tree, peppermint, lavender, or eucalyptus with the wardrobe spray can help keep things smelling fresh, but you will want to make absolutely sure that nobody has a sensitivity or allergy before doing that. Personally, I do not mix essential oils into my wardrobe spray.

For spraying costume pieces, you will want to have each piece hung individually on a hanger in the dressing room. I try to encourage performers to do this at the end of the night to make the wardrobe crew's work easier. I spray

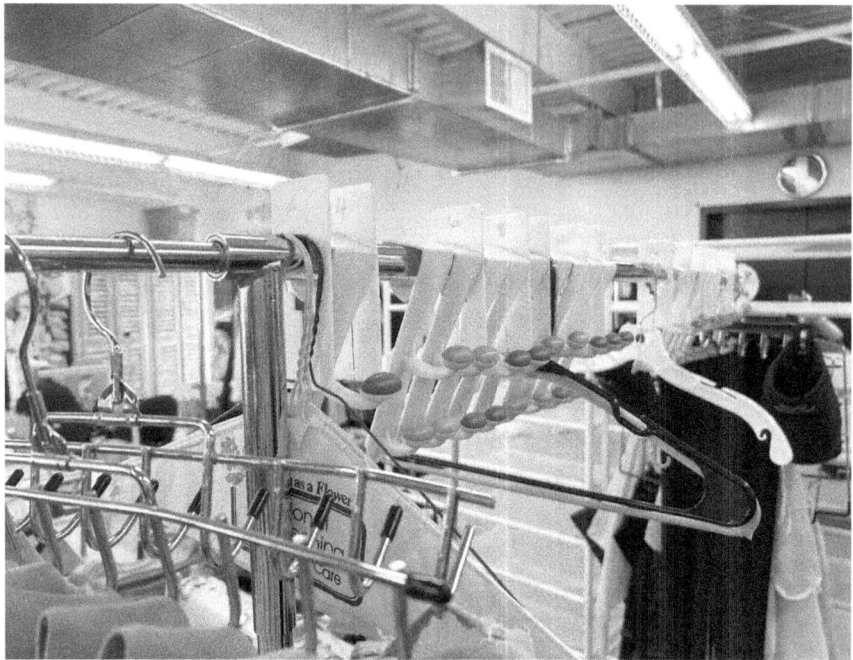

Figure 7.2 The hooks hung on a garment rack labeled with corresponding numbers for hang drying items at The Phoenix Theatre Company.

Photograph taken by the author.

the inside of the garment in the areas most likely to be sweaty and have odor. For tops, this is often the armpit and neck areas. For bottoms, it is the inside of the waistband and crotch. One to three sprays per garment is plenty, as you do not want to oversaturate the garment. Then try to spread the garments out on the rack so that they aren't touching each other, as the air circulation will help them to dry prior to the next performance. If any items are particularly wet from sweat, hanging them over a box fan can help them to dry out.

If shoes or other accessories in the show begin to become odorous, you will need to disinfect them to kill the bacteria that is causing the odor. Many products are commercially available, including deodorizer balls, powders, and charcoal bags. I have always used Lysol™ spray and sprayed once in each shoe on the inside. However, some people are allergic to Lysol™ and other aerosols, so if this is the case which anyone on the crew or in the cast, you will need to try one of the other methods.

You should do the laundry after each performance so that line-dry items have time to dry before the next performance. When you arrive for the next performance, you may need to fluff items in the dryer for a few minutes before distributing them. You will then hang or fold the items and place hanging items back into the mesh bags and distribute the laundry into the dressing rooms for each performer, so it is there when the performers arrive to get dressed. If you are following Actor's Equity Association or other union rules, the time that costumes must be made available will be mandated. It is often at the half-hour call, meaning a half hour prior to the start of the show.

The next important maintenance step is pressing and steaming. You will want to confirm with the costume designer during the dress rehearsal process if there are pieces that do not need to be pressed or steamed. Sometimes if the look of a character is distressed or their character's personality is not neat, the designer will prefer that you do not press or steam the costumes for that performer. Having a list of which pieces get pressed, which get steamed, and which do not get either will be helpful for you and your crew as you formulate your preshow routines. Pressing (ironing) is best done with a traditional ironing board. This is the preferred method for pants, dress shirts, and some skirts. Steaming is a huge timesaver and is preferred for dresses, blazers, suit coats, knit garments, robes, and other large or flowy items. The most important thing to know about steaming is that it requires tension on the top and bottom of the garment to work well. You should hang the costume piece from the steamer's hanger hook or an elevated position and then pull down on the bottom of the garment as you go. The steamer wand should be placed on the inside of the garment wherever possible, and you should work from top to bottom to remove wrinkles. Be aware that garment steamers can cause burns and use a heat-resistant glove if needed. If an area is too small to fit the steamer wand inside (such as a sleeve), steaming from the outside is acceptable, again working from top to bottom and providing tension by pulling down on the bottom of the sleeve or other area. Some of your pressing items may also require the use of starch. Starch helps stiffen things such as collars and cuffs and should be used for items that need a stiff look. It is important to press or steam costume pieces prior to each performance, particularly items that have obvious wrinkles or are rumpled from the dryer. Developing an efficient pre-show pressing and steaming routine for your team is an essential part of costume maintenance. In cases where this would require too many hours for the wardrobe team and they would go into overtime, some organizations choose to employ a separate costume maintenance or prep crew. If you work somewhere where this happens, be sure to coordinate with the other crew to have repair issues addressed and items laundered and prepped for each performance, and how communication about these matters will take place. Sometimes the personnel hired for a prep crew may not have strong stitching skills. If this is the case, you may want them to focus more on steaming, pressing, reattaching jewelry or other items that were removed for washing, distributing laundry, and taking costumes to their location for the beginning of the show. If the prep crew is pressing and steaming, ask them to check seams, hems, and closures as they go and make a note of any issues that they discover so that the wardrobe crew can perform repairs as necessary. Developing a clear system on how wardrobe crew will communicate prep and laundry needs to the maintenance team and how they will communicate costume pieces that need repaired back to the wardrobe team is important so that the costumes can be properly taken care of and prepped for every performance.

Repairs are a large part of the wardrobe team's workload. Some repairs are small, such as a button falling off or a hem coming unsewn. Some repairs are larger such as a tear in the fabric. Repairs can also include accessories such as hats, jewelry, or shoes. Familiarizing yourself with basic sewing techniques and alterations, craft skills, and shoe repair will serve you well as a wardrobe supervisor. One technique to familiarize yourself with is machine and hand darning. This method will help repair a tear in a costume piece and keep you from having to replace the piece entirely. Fishnet stockings tend to snag often and can be hand darned with matching elastic thread. If you are unsure of the best way to fix something, you should communicate with the costume shop manager or costume staff to find out. If a shoe repair is beyond your capabilities, you may want to take it to a cobbler to be professionally fixed. You should ask the costume staff for a wardrobe repair kit for each production. This would include things like extra fabric, spare buttons, excess trim, matching thread, and more for use in small repairs. Repair work can sometimes include making small alterations if the way a costume piece fits a performer changes throughout the run. The alteration should only be done to preserve the intended fit of the costume and its functionality, not to change the fit that the designer and their team intended.

Maintenance requires keeping things looking like they did when the show first opens. If tights were dyed a particular color and they are fading with laundering, you may need to give them another dip in the dye pot. Extra fabric dye and a recipe should be included with your wardrobe kit. If shoes were painted for the production but they are getting scuffed with the choreography, you will need to touch them up. Shoe paint should be included in your kit with recipes if colors were mixed. Jewelry pieces may lose their sheen over time and require polishing and cleaning. Trim may start to fray or wear and should be replaced if extra trim was provided. Finding ways to keep the costumes looking like new is an important part of maintaining the integrity of the costume design and will serve you well as a wardrobe supervisor.

DAILY WIG MAINTENANCE

As discussed in Chapter 6, many productions will employ professionals skilled in wig design and maintenance. In smaller venues, daily wig maintenance may fall to the wardrobe team, so it is important to familiarize yourself with the basic skills necessary for this function.

The biggest element in daily wig maintenance is to return the wigs to a head block and perform the process of blocking. Blocking a wig is the process of sitting the wig on the block properly, so it is centered, and no part of the wig is folded under or wrinkled. You will then take bias tape (I prefer the single fold, ½" wide in a neutral color) and wet it. You want the piece to be long enough to cover the entire front hairline of the wig lace, from ear to ear over the top. Starting in the center, at the top of the head, you will use straight, ball-head pins to secure the bias tape through the lace to the head block. Canvas head blocks work best for this, but if you only have foam available, it will work. Working down from the center, moving from top to bottom, and working back and forth from side to side (right to left), you will stretch the wet bias tape over the edge of the wig lace, securing it with pins as you go. You should stagger the pins, so one is higher, and the next one is lower, so that if the lace starts to rip a little, the other pin is higher, and it won't rip further. Make sure you are NOT stretching the wig lace, and if it has begun to bubble, stretch, or show signs of wear, attempt to force it back into its correct shape on the head and use the wet bias tape to help get it back into shape. The wet bias tape will have some stretch to it, so pulling on it as you pin it in place will help to reshape the lace edge appropriately. With as many pins as necessary, complete this process for the entire front of the hairline, going from the center down towards the sideburn, then up the sideburn to the ear (see Figure 7.3). This process helps keep the wig lace from getting stretched or damaged from wearing.

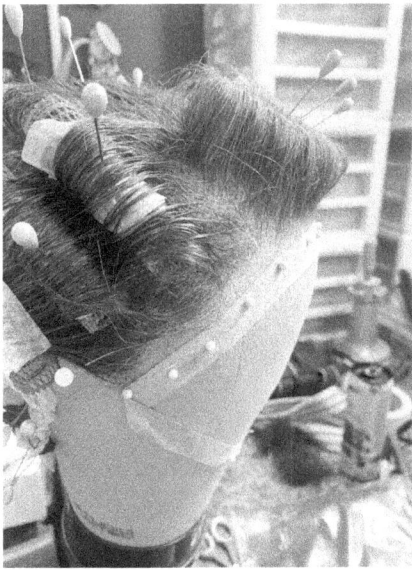 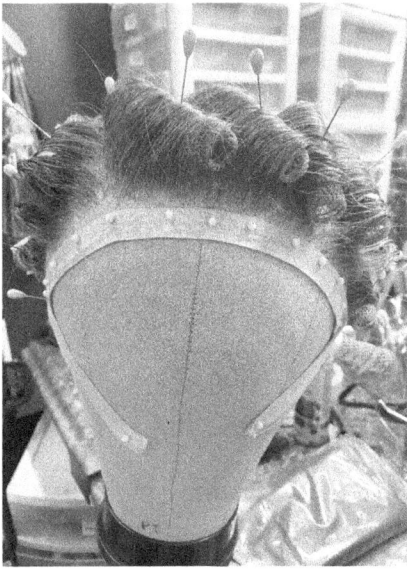

Figure 7.3 A wig with a roller set that is blocked using bias tape. Front and side view. Photograph compliments of Kelly Yurko.

Depending on the style, a mesh-style hairnet can be put on the wig after blocking. This will keep styles that are curled from uncurling and going limp. Gravity and drying sweat can take the life out of a curled style, but hairnets can help relieve the effect of gravity and keep the curls intact longer. If the curls continue losing their shape, but you can still see how the hair was curled when styled, you can use rollers or large duckbill clips to re-curl the pieces as pictured in Figure 7.4. You can do this after the show, hopefully while waiting for the washing machine to finish, and then take the clips or rollers out prior to the next performance.

If the production uses artificial facial hair, sometimes that requires maintenance as well. The proper tools for styling facial hair are thermal stoves and

Figure 7.4 A wig with curls being retouched with various-sized rollers, roller clips, and duckbill clips.
Photograph taken by the author.

Figure 7.5 A stove iron heating up inside a thermal stove.
Photograph taken by Kelly Yurko.

stove irons as pictured in Figure 7.5. The diameter is much smaller than most commercial curling irons and they are kept hot by heating the ends in the stove. The pointed ends can be used to restore texture and shape to the facial hair, being careful not to burn yourself.

Learning to properly maintain wigs and facial hair could be an entire book unto itself, but the information offered here is meant as a starting point for wardrobe professionals who find themselves responsible for daily wig upkeep. Touching up wigs and facial hair throughout the process will help keep them from needing to be fully reset as often. If you can observe or work with a wig master at any point, I recommend learning as much as possible.

CHAPTER 8

Next Steps

STRIKE

Isn't a strike when you walk off the job and stop working? Not in the world of theatre. Strike is what happens after the closing performance of a production. All the departments do everything necessary to restore the venue to its original condition. The scenic crew takes down all of the set pieces and either disposes of them, dismantles them, or relocates them to storage. The lighting team takes down any lights hung specifically for the production and often restores the venue's rep plot as required. All areas are cleared of show-related materials and cleaned. The stage is often repainted, usually matte black.

Wardrobe department strike differs greatly for all types of venues and companies. Prior to strike, confirm with your supervisor exactly which duties you and your team will be responsible for as part of strike. Once you understand your responsibilities, you should come up with a strike plan, which will help you lead your team through the process and keep things moving along efficiently. Remember that strike often comes at the end of a long week of performances and possibly a very long show run; crew members can be worn out. Being specific about what needs to be accomplished before the end of strike will help everyone stay focused and work effectively.

Strike can range anywhere from a couple of hours to multiple days or even weeks. If you are a union member or working with a hired crew that is being paid a particular day rate, there will be a set number of hours allowed for a strike call and overtime may not be a possibility. Devising a strike plan that is achievable within the time limit is an important part of your planning.

What should be included in a strike plan and where should you start? Your main goals are:

1. Clean the costumes.
2. Sanitize the accessories (such as shoes and hats).
3. Sort the dry cleaning.
4. Empty and clean the dressing rooms.
5. Remove wardrobe-related items from the backstage areas.
6. Organize the wardrobe room/area.
7. Restock costume pieces and accessories once they are cleaned/sanitized.

Adding additional items to your strike plan or removing any of the above will depend on what is happening to the costumes after the production. Is it a rental that is being returned? Is it becoming a rental package, and does it need to be stored and labeled in a particular way? Are the costumes being returned to the costume stock of the theater where you are working? Whatever the case may be, you will want to know the answers to these questions prior to strike so that you can plan appropriately.

If any or all of the costumes were rented, you will want to confirm with the rental company or the person at your company who has the rental information whether or not the costumes need to be cleaned prior to being returned. You will also want to confirm the rental return deadline. Some rental companies prefer costumes to be returned dirty and charge a cleaning fee, while others require everything to be cleaned and for you to provide proof of purchase for dry cleaning. Find out whether the rental return deadline is the ship by or receive by date. This will help you plan how long you have to get all the rented items boxed up and shipped out (or returned locally if you are lucky enough to have a local source for costume rentals). Some rental companies also require that any name labels inside of costumes or accessories that you added are removed prior to rental return, so this task could be a part of the strike process.

A good order of operations for a strike call could be:

1. Sort and start as many loads of laundry as possible, depending on the number of machines available. If costume pieces have makeup stains on the collar or other stains that have built up over the run, try to use stain removers and some elbow grease to get them as clean as possible.
2. Sort items that need to be dry cleaned and put them in large bags or bundle with fabric ties for transport.
3. Remove all items from the dressing rooms. Sort accessories into categories (for example, glasses, hats, jewelry, shoes, etc.).

4. Sanitize the accessories (such as shoes and hats). Spray the inside of hats and shoes with disinfectant spray to kill bacteria (but first confirm nobody working the strike call has an allergy to this).
5. Empty and clean the dressing rooms. Wipe down mirrors and surfaces. Sweep and mop.
6. Remove rack tags from dressing rooms and wardrobe areas. Remove show-related labels from rack tags and ditty bags. Remove wardrobe-related paperwork from dressing rooms.
7. Remove wardrobe-related items and paperwork from backstage areas. Clean these areas.
8. Organize the wardrobe room/area.
9. Restock or pack costume pieces and accessories once they are clean/sanitized.

While working through the list, laundry should be the first priority. As soon as a load finishes, switch it to the dryer or hang dry/flat dry any items that cannot go in the dryer. Start another load of wash immediately. There is often a lot of laundry to do at a strike, and the facilities do not usually have enough machines, so keeping things moving through the laundry as quickly as possible is important. There may also be items that need to be handwashed. Sort these items and have one of your crew members begin handwashing items during the first step. If there is a lot of handwashing, have additional crew members assist or have them swap out so one person doesn't end up doing handwashing for too long.

When you are making your strike plan, estimate how many loads of laundry there will be and how much time each load takes. Are there additional items that will be washed, such as hanging bags, mesh bags, garment bags, or accessories? Include all of these items in your estimates so that you can get an idea of how long the strike will take. If you are working within a limited time for strike, plan how much of the laundry will be doable within the allotted time and make a plan for how the rest of the laundry will be done. You do not want to start a load of laundry in the washer if strike is ending in 30 minutes. Creating a spreadsheet that denotes when the costume pieces are "dead" (meaning they are not worn again) throughout the show is a helpful part of the strike plan. If crew members have time during the show or at intermission, they could wash a load of dead costume pieces, which will reduce the amount of laundry to be done post-show. The chart in Figure 8.1 was created by Lucinda Koenig for one of The Phoenix Theatre Company's productions. She notes when the items are "dead" during Act 1, at intermission, or post-show. She also lists the washing instruction abbreviations next to the item for easy reference and lists the dry-cleaning items separately so they can be pulled out. A chart like this is a great way to organize your strike laundry schedule.

116   THE WARDROBE SUPERVISOR'S TOOLKIT

Show Title
Laundry - Final Show

	DEAD DURING ACT 1		DEAD @ INTERMISSION		DEAD POST SHOW
Actor 1	Grey Stripe Shirt (MW/TDL)	Actor 2	Black/Grey Raglan Tee (MW(io)/TDL)	Actor 2	Blue/Red Stripe Boxers (MW/TDL)
Actor 1	Tan Stripe Sweater (GW/DF)	Actor 2	Black Denim Shorts (MW/TDL)	Actor 2	Black Hoodie (MW/TDL)
Actor 2	Blue/Olive Plaid Shirt (MW/TDL)	Actor 2	White Thermal Pants (MW/TDL)	Actor 2	Black Sweat Bands (MW/TDL)
Actor 2	Brown Print Tee (MW(io)/TDL)	Actor 4	Black Denim Corset Top (GW(io)/HD)	Actor 2	Charcoal Tank Top (MW/TDL)
Actor 2	Jeans (MW/TDL)	Actor 6	Black/Tan Edge Head Scarf (HW/TDL)*in bag	Actor 2	Olive Track Pants (MW/TDL)
Actor 3	Green Jacket (MW/TDL)	Actor 8	Blue Pinstripe Suit Pants (GW/HD)	Actor 2	Olive Track Pants (MW/TDL)
Actor 3	Jeans (MW/TDL)	Actor 8	Distressed Denim Shorts (MW(io)/TDL)	Actor 2	Camo Jacket (MW/TDL)
Actor 3	White MC Magic Tee (MW(io)/TDL)	Actor 1	Blue Stripe Shirt (MW/TDL) * collar stays	Actor 10	Denim Jacket (MW/TDL)
Actor 4	Coral Shirt (MW/TDL)	Actor 1	Charcoal Pants (MW/TDL)	Actor 10	Brown Dress (MW/TDL)
Actor 4	Olive Vest (MW/TDL)	Actor 13	Cream Shirt (MW/TDL)	Actor 10	Yellow Leggings (MW/TDL)
Actor 4	Teal Corduroy Skirt (GW/HD)	Actor 13	Navy/Green Argyle Sweater Vest (GW(io)/TDL)	Actor 11	Blue Dress (GW(io)/TDL)
Actor 4	Yellow/Blue Tie Dye Tights (HW/HD)	Actor 6	Green/Blue Chevron Wrap Dress (GW/TDL)	Actor 11	Rose Leggins (MW(io)/TDL)
Actor 5	Navy/Pink Stripe Dress (GW/HD)	Actor 6	Dark Brown Pant (GW/TDL)	Actor 11	Denim Jacket (MW/TDL)
Actor 5	Tan/Multi Stripe Sweater (HW/HD)	Actor 8	White Shirt (MW/TDL)	Actor 4	Black Print Romper (MW/HD)
Actor 6	Purple/Multi Texture Dress (HW/HD)	Actor 5	Teal Sweater Dress (HW/DF)	Actor 1	Violet Stripe Shirt (MW/HD)
Actor 6	Navy Cardigan (GW/TDL)	Actor 5	Burgundy Boot Sock Top (MW/TDL)*in bag	Actor 13	Navy Pants (MW/TDL)
Actor 7	Black Leather Jacket (GW/LD)	Actor 5	Red Floral Scarf (HW/TDL)*in bag	Actor 13	Green Plaid Shirt (MW/TDL)
Actor 7	Black Ramones Tee (MW(io)/TDL)	Actor 3	Blue/Red/White Stripe Shirt (MW/TDL)	Actor 6	Navy Paisley Skirt (GW/HD)
Actor 8	Brown Stripe Shirt (MW/TDL)	Actor 3	Navy Pants (MW/TDL)	Actor 6	Navy Tank (MW/TDL)
Actor 8	Dark Brown/Star Waistband Pants (HW/HD)	Actor 6	Blue Henley (GW/TDL)	Actor 6	Plum Cardigan (GW/TDL)
Actor 8	Grey Stripe Tee (MW/TDL)	Actor 9	Blue Plaid Boxers (MW/TDL)	Actor 6	Navy Head Scarf (HW/TDL)*in bag
Actor 9	Plaid Scarf (GW/HD)*in bag	Actor 9	Grey Suit Pants (MW/TDL)	Actor 8	Light Blue Stripe Shirt (MW/TDL)
Actor 9	Levi Signature Jeans (MW/TDL)	Actor 7	White Sleeveless Shirt (GW/TDL)	Actor 8	Burgundy Tee (MW/TDL)
Actor 10	White Print Robe (MW/TDL)	Actor 14	Burgundy Obey Tee (MW/TDL)	Actor 7	Tan Pants (MW(io)/TDL)
Actor 10	Blue PJ Bottom (GW(io)/TDL)	Actor 14	Jeans (MW/TDL)	Actor 5	White/Black Stripe Shirt (GW/TDL)
Actor 12	Blue PJ Top (GW(io)/TDL)	Actor 12	Burgundy Fringed Floral Scarf (HW/HD) *in bag	Actor 5	Red Pleated Skirt (HW/HD)
Actor 11	Blue PJ Bottom (GW(io)/TDL)	Actor 12	Tan Boot Top Sock (GW/TDL)*in bag	Actor 5	Green Scarf (HW/TDL)*in bag
Actor 11	Navy PJ Top (GW(io)/TDL)	Actor 12	Green Floral Skirt (HW/HD)	Actor 5	Black/White Apple Print Dress (HW/DF)
Actor 11	White Print Robe (MW/TDL)	Actor 12	Rust Mauve Sweater (HW/HD)	Actor 5	Denim Jacket (MW/TDL)
		Actor 12	Mauve Tank (HW/DF)	Actor 3	Grey Suit Pants (MW/TDL)
				Actor 3	White Shirt (MW/TDL)
	Dry Clean			Actor 9	White/Grey/Blue Plaid Shirt (GW/TDL)
Actor 2	Grey Hoodie Vest			Actor 9	Grey Tee (MW/TDL)
Actor 9	Brown Corduroy Jacket			Actor 9	Levis 511 Jeans (MW/TDL)
Actor 12	Grey Suit Jacket			Actor 7	Red/Yellow/Blue Plaid Shirt (MW/TDL)
Actor 13	Rust Jacket			Actor 7	Tan Jacket (GW/HD)
Actor 4	Wool Jacket			Actor 7	Jeans (MW(io)/TDL)
Actor 4	Velvet Burnout Opera Jacket			Actor 14	Blue Lucky 13 Tee (MW(io)/TDL)
Actor 9	Grey Plaid Reversible Vest			Actor 14	Corduroy Jeans (MW/TDL)
Actor 8	Blue Pinstripe Suit Jacket			Actor 14	Plaid Scarf (HW/TDL)*in bag
Actor 8	Grey Suit Vest			Actor 12	Navy Janis Joplin Tee (MW/TDL)
Actor 7	Navy/Lavender Suit Jacket			Actor 12	Tan/Blue Print Shirt (GW/DF)
Actor 7	Navy/Lavender Suit Pants			Actor 12	Mustard Dot Cardigan (MW/HD)
Actor 1	Navy Vest			Actor 13	Cream Cable Knit Sweater (HW/DF)
Actor 3	Grey Green Pants			Actor 9	Navy Cardigan (HW/␣)
Actor 3	Grey Suit Jacket				
Actor 3	Grey Suit Vest				
Actor 14	Brown Corduroy Jacket	$40.00			
16 lbs.					

Figure 8.1 A chart created for strike listing when costume pieces are "dead" created by Lucinda Koenig for The Phoenix Theatre Company

If restocking the costumes and accessories is part of your team's responsibilities, that can either be part of the initial strike or take place in the days following the final performance. Depending on if the costume and accessory storage is onsite or not can impact the logistics of this. Where I currently work, accessories are stored onsite, but the costume and shoe storage is across campus in a building that is not accessible on the weekends. At the strike call after the final performance, the crew will sort, disinfect, and restock the accessories while sorting the shoes and costume pieces into bags and baskets to be transported to storage. In the days following the final performance, costume shop staff will assist me with transporting the items to storage and restocking them.

There is always the issue of dry cleaning with a wardrobe strike. The largest number of costume pieces is usually what is sent after the final performance, so it can take some extra time for the dry cleaner to get everything clean. You will want to find out when the dry cleaning will be ready and try to arrange to have some approved labor hours for crew to help you unload and restock everything from the dry cleaner. There is nothing worse than having to make multiple trips from your car to the costume storage with all of the freshly cleaned costume pieces and then restock all of them by yourself. Something inevitably falls on the ground or on the stairs and it can be exhausting. This is a key issue for costume/wardrobe strike, because a bit of the timeline is out of our control. Other departments or the production manager may not understand that the costume strike can go on for a week or two, depending on dry cleaning and rentals.

The keys to an effective wardrobe strike are understanding your responsibilities, estimating the amount and duration of laundry, identifying handwash and dry clean only items, devising a plan to keep all crew members busy, prioritizing switching over the laundry, and leaving the venue in the condition you found it in (or better). With proper planning, clear communication, and effective leadership, you can make the strike process a successful achievement for you and your team.

RENTAL RETURNS

If any or all of the costume pieces for your production were rented, it is very important to return them to the rental company properly to avoid incurring any fines for the company you are working for. Rental companies will provide instructions for rental returns. Be sure to read everything multiple times to ensure that you understand everything they require. One company I rented from required that all costume pieces be wrapped in plastic prior to being placed inside the box in case any water got into the box. Some shipping companies require that boxes be new, not reused. Paperwork or an inventory may need to be included in each box. If I am involved with rentals that are being shipped, I try to be the one that unpacks the boxes when they arrive if possible. If this is not possible, I will ask whoever is unpacking the boxes to take pictures as they go so that I know how everything was packed. Even if I am the one unpacking them, I will also take pictures so I can reference them when I am packing them for return. If an inventory of each box is provided, check it off as you unpack the boxes to be sure that everything listed is actually in that box. If a box-by-box inventory is not available, make one as you unpack the boxes or indicate on the master inventory which box everything is in (numbering the boxes starting with #1). There is no such thing as too much information when it comes to rentals. When using rental items alongside theater stock items, it is useful to create a labeling system to help differentiate the source of each item. I have done this by cutting small pieces of colored ribbon that I attach to a hidden part of the costume, such as the inside of a pocket with a small brass safety pin. If costumes have been rented or borrowed from more than one company, I will use a different color ribbon for each source. This can help during strike to easily identify the pieces that need to be returned to a rental house.

When packing the costumes for rental return, follow the rental company's instructions exactly. Even if they do not ask to wrap things in plastic, it isn't a bad idea to protect the pieces. Take pictures as you pack the boxes and check off on your list every item as you pack it, so that at the end you will know for sure that all of the items are in the boxes. Use a reputable shipping company that provides tracking information and be sure to use appropriate insurance for the replacement cost of the items if they were to get lost or damaged in transport. Provide the tracking information to the rental company along with the estimated date of arrival so that they know when to expect the costumes to arrive. Confirm that the company receives the items and do this via email so that you have confirmation in writing that they arrived. Following the instructions for a rental return is very important so that you do not incur any unnecessary charges and to keep you and your company's relationship with the rental company a positive one.

COSTUME STOCK ORGANIZATION

Costume stock organization is a topic that requires its own toolkit and is approached differently by every theatre company in the world. However, understanding a few basic principles is helpful for wardrobe professionals whose responsibilities may include restocking items. My golden rule of costume stock organization is "***you must put things away in the right place, otherwise, you should just throw them away***". This may sound a tad dramatic, but it is true, especially the larger the costume inventory. The costume storage area at The Phoenix Theatre Company is large and very well organized, as seen in Figure 8.2. If someone is rushing and restocks a pair of dance shoes in with the rain boots because there is an empty spot and the container is on a lower shelf, it could be years before another person looks in there and finds them. Unfortunately, in the meantime, those dance shoes may have been needed for a show and the missing item creates an unnecessary expense for the company. Restocking costumes can be tedious and unpleasant, but taking the time to ensure that you are putting things away in the correct places is crucial.

If a production creates a new group of costumes that does not currently exist in the costume stock (such as tabards for a medieval play), you will want to discuss with the costume shop staff and all of those who utilize the costume stock where the best place to store the new item will be. If you are restocking and have items that you do not know the proper storage spot for, ask the others and determine the best location. Try not to guess and do not put something somewhere just to get it away if you are not sure that is where it goes. When costume designers are pulling from stock for their production, they do not have time to look at every single piece in stock, so they will be looking in categories and bins that should contain the items they need. If the stock has those items, but they are not in places where one could reasonably expect to find them, then they might as well be lost or thrown away.

Another thing to think about when restocking is sizing. It is much faster to pull a pair of pants from a section containing the waist size and inseam length you need as opposed to looking through hundreds of pairs of pants and possibly having to measure many of them, only to discover that stock does not contain the size or type of pant you are looking for. The same holds true for dress shirts, dresses, suits, outerwear, shoes, and more. To the best of your ability, given the size of your storage space and the number of costume pieces and accessories stored there, try to organize items by type/category and then by size. Figure 8.3 depicts shoe storage bins at The Phoenix Theatre Company. Taking the time to do the extra step of sizing will save hours of time for those pulling from the stock later. Again, placing items in their proper size range section is crucial when your stock is organized by size, or else the items will not be used because those pulling will not know that the item is an option if it is miscategorized.

There are a couple of other things to keep in mind when restocking costumes. Costumes should be clean and dry before restocking them. Moisture, sunlight, and heat are the enemies of clothing. Your costume storage area should not have windows, and if it does, you will want to make light-blocking curtains for it and consider rack covers for hanging racks and storage bins that are not clear to keep the sunlight from damaging items. If the storage area is humid at all, you will want to install dehumidifiers and other air treatments to keep the air cool and dry. Do not store costumes in a facility that is not climate-controlled.

Figure 8.2 Costume storage at The Phoenix Theatre Company. Photograph taken by the author.

Do not crush the hats! Hats are often stored in bins or hat boxes. Sometimes they are stored hanging up on the wall on nails or hooks. Hanging is a great storage option for hats if you have the space, but they can get dusty depending on the location. Wrapping them in plastic or having sheets or something to drape over them to protect them from dust can be helpful. If the hats are stored in bins or boxes, do not overfill the box and do not stuff them in. Some hats can be stacked on top of each other and nested together if the size and style can accommodate that. Jamming too many hats into a bin and shoving the lid on can result in hats that are too damaged to be worn. Hats can be an expensive investment for a company, so keeping them in good condition is important.

Figure 8.3 Shoe and accessory storage in The Phoenix Theatre Company's costume stock. Photograph taken by the author.

Costume stock organization can be an important part of a wardrobe professional's job responsibilities. Taking the time to ensure you are putting things away properly and in the correct place can help save time and money down the road. Working collaboratively with the costume shop staff and designers who utilize the stock to constantly improve its organization will benefit all. Even if restocking and organizing is not your favorite part of the job, doing it well can be rewarding and will be appreciated by those you work with.

CREATING A RECORD

As discussed at length in Chapter 3, creating a record for the production is an important part of the wardrobe supervisor's job. Much like stage managers creating a prompt book for each production they manage, the wardrobe supervisor should do the same. Much of this can now be created digitally, and you will want to ensure all of the people that could need to access the paperwork in the future have the permissions that they need. This includes saving final copies of the paperwork onto a company-administered share drive and labeling them appropriately so they can be referenced in the future. Even if you do not think a show will ever be remounted, it is good practice to create a record of the work your team did on the show.

Your record should include run sheets, laundry schedules, dressing/piece lists, and any additional paperwork created for the production. These items could be referenced if the show is remounted but can also be helpful if a similar size project is being produced because you will be able to see how many wardrobe crew members worked on the show and how busy their tracks were. You can estimate dry cleaning costs and laundry/cleaning needs from past paperwork. You could even create a tracking sheet of how much consumable products are used per show (for example, detergent, dryer sheets, stain remover, wardrobe spray, lint rollers, etc.) and reference this when purchasing supplies for future productions.

Keeping your paperwork updated and in good order after a production is also beneficial for you as you move through your wardrobe career. If you are interviewing for a job, they will often want to see samples of paperwork that you have created, and having final copies of examples at your fingertips will make that process much easier. As you build a collection of paperwork samples, you can upload some of them to your professional website to send to potential employers. Examples of your organizational and paperwork skills are an important part of your professional portfolio.

You may find yourself working for a company where you are the primary Wardrobe Supervisor, but the company operates multiple spaces and the productions overlap, so they may hire additional Wardrobe Supervisors for individual productions. This is similar to how a Production Stage Manager functions and collaborates with the Stage Manager for each production. This makes you more of a Director of Wardrobe, where the ultimate responsibility from the company's standpoint still falls to you. Because you work for the company full-time, you can work as an intermediary between the costume designer and costume shop staff and the wardrobe supervisor. If possible, you can be there throughout the tech process to show the wardrobe supervisor the ropes and help put out theoretical fires that may arise throughout the tech process. This process will require you to give up ownership of a show and become comfortable with delegating while maintaining responsibility. This can be challenging but is ultimately a great skill to add to your management toolbox. You may still build the paperwork and run sheets but updating them will fall to the wardrobe supervisor. This can also be a great dynamic for the wardrobe supervisor, especially if they are new to the company, because they can blame you for things that cast members do not like. This allows them to build a rapport with the cast and still maintain the integrity of the costume design.

Creating a record that can be accessed by those in the company who might need to reference it in the future is also an act of goodwill. The live production industry is, as we always say, "a small world" where everyone knows each other, and you will often get jobs based on who you know. The same is true if an employer has a bad relationship with you. If you are applying for a job with a new company and someone at that company knows someone from a previous job you had where you were not a good employee, that can ruin your chance for the new position. Therefore, always try to leave a good impression on everyone you work with. You never know when a kind word about you will make the difference or when someone mentioning your name will open a door for you. Although there are situations that may not be good working environments, try not to burn bridges whenever possible.

CHAPTER 9

Teaching Wardrobe

TEACHING PHILOSOPHY

Many universities and colleges have excellent theatre departments that produce amazing shows. Unfortunately, one thing that many institutions lack is formal training in wardrobe. Most institutions do not have anyone on faculty or staff to mentor or train the wardrobe crew and students are often left to figure it out on their own. Other times the costuming staff or faculty are stretched thin by all of the responsibilities, which can include hair and makeup, and no one has time to train students in wardrobe. Although there is value in figuring things out on your own, there is also immense value in wardrobe training. There are also very few classes about wardrobe or classes that touch on wardrobe in any aspect of the curriculum. As I discovered when planning a course in costume shop and wardrobe management, there were absolutely zero texts on the subject of wardrobe for live performance (and thus the proposal for this book was born). Developing a plan to train students in wardrobe is a very valuable endeavor and can offer graduates a sustainable avenue for income.

One of the most important aspects of wardrobe training involves ownership and accountability. Empowering the wardrobe supervisor and their crew to feel responsible for how each performer looks when they step onstage is essential. This starts with assigning one student as a wardrobe supervisor and the rest of the students as the wardrobe crew. If it is a very large production, an assistant wardrobe supervisor could also be assigned. Depending on the needs of the production, the crew could be assigned to individual performers or to each side of the stage and backstage location. For pre-show work including laundry, pressing, and steaming, assigning individual crew members to a set of performers or an entire dressing room is an effective way to divide the work. Also, it gives each crew member accountability for their assigned performers or room. They should be responsible for distributing the laundry, checking in the costume pieces, and preparing all of the pieces by pressing and steaming. Each crew member should then do the presets backstage of any costume pieces they will need for costume changes during the show or for performers that they are responsible for, even if the performer will do the costume change themselves.

Depending on the number of crew assigned and the size of the show, the wardrobe supervisor should be encouraged to delegate as many of the costume changes and other duties during the show as possible. This allows them to supervise as much as possible and be available to solve problems that come up during the show. If a quick-change is not going well, the wardrobe supervisor can step in to help get it back on track. If a costume piece malfunctions, they can attempt a quick fix to make it wearable. If an accessory is missing, they can try to locate it quickly. By delegating as much as possible and giving each crew member specific assignments, the supervisor can give each crew member a sense of ownership, which is incredibly important. Once crew members are responsible for specific things, it is easier to hold them accountable when things go wrong and improvements need to be made. Some wardrobe crews will be small and their responsibilities so great that it will be impossible for the wardrobe supervisor to delegate as much as would be preferable. The supervisor will have their own track with responsibilities for pre-show duties, presets, quick-changes, tracking, and post-show duties. The supervisor should avoid the temptation to assign themselves to the busiest or most complicated track, thus allowing them time for problem solving and double-checking things.

One of the challenges for educators in this type of training is the balance between letting students fail in order to learn and offering them the guidance needed to succeed. It can be nearly impossible to stand back and watch a quick-change going wrong and not intervene, but sometimes failure is necessary for the students to learn how to get it right. Offering suggestions of what to improve or modifications to the process will help the students find the path to success, but stepping in and doing it yourself may not. Ensuring that enough time is built into the tech and dress rehearsal process to allow for this learning to occur is essential. Scheduling quick-change rehearsals and crew training sessions and meetings prior to the dress rehearsals can help newer wardrobe crew members to feel confident about their skills when the pressure is on.

A counterintuitive approach to wardrobe training requires the teacher to remove themselves from the situation. For example, at my current institution, we have three nights of dress rehearsals. On the first night, I spend most of the night backstage and in the dressing rooms with the wardrobe crew, answering questions and instructing them on where to go and how to do things. On the second night, I am there, but I try not to talk very much and only answer questions as they come up. I also observe and offer feedback either when things are happening or after the rehearsal, depending on the situation. On the third night, I let my crew know that I will not be backstage, but rather watching the show from the house. During pre-show, I usually leave the building all together, but the crew is able to contact me on my cell phone in case of an emergency. This scaffolded approach to mentorship allows the student wardrobe supervisor to be empowered to lead the team, while also learning how to do the job throughout the process. I am often amazed by the ways the students solve problems when I remove myself from the situation. They do not always come up with the same solution I would have offered, but they find a way to keep the show moving and I can always offer them advice and alternate solutions later. This method also encourages the performers to respect the student wardrobe supervisor and their crew and ask them questions and communicate important information with them instead of always coming to the faculty or staff.

Empowering the students who are leading and working on the wardrobe crew is essential to good wardrobe training. If students end up working in wardrobe professionally, that accountability and responsibility will be an important part of their success. Learning to solve problems quickly and stay calm under pressure can only happen by navigating stressful situations successfully. I am not a proponent of "throwing students into the deep end" without guidance or mentorship, but I do propose offering them a level of autonomy before they feel 100% ready. They will often surprise themselves (and maybe their mentors too) with their leadership and problem-solving skills when given the chance to use them.

PRACTICAL EXPERIENCE

It is actually not too surprising that there are not many classes that cover wardrobe, because wardrobe skills can only be learned by doing. It would be nearly impossible to recreate the show conditions necessary to hone wardrobe skills effectively. If a class could be offered, it could cover paperwork creation, all the steps to prepare for a production, how to run a production, costume maintenance and preparation, methods for quick-changes, and more, and it would be very helpful for students wishing to pursue

Figure 9.1 A student wardrobe supervisor and two members of the wardrobe crew look at paperwork for a production at Albright College.
Photograph taken by John Pankratz, Ph.D.

professional wardrobe opportunities. However, nothing can substitute the practical experience of working on the wardrobe crew for a production. Practical experience is essential for students interested in learning and improving wardrobe skills. It allows students to experience the pressure of a live performance and requires them to think on their feet and stay calm in stressful situations. By navigating the various problems that arise throughout the run of a show, students will apply all that they have learned and learn so much more.

Depending on the size of the crew and the needs of the production, the wardrobe crew can even be split into a wardrobe crew and a maintenance crew. Especially in educational institutions, this can be a helpful solution to student burnout and fatigue. For this method, both crews are assigned a supervisor, a wardrobe supervisor, and a maintenance supervisor. Then they are each assigned crew members. The wardrobe crew does the costume check-ins, pre-show preparations and presets, runs the show, sprays the costumes with wardrobe spray, and collects the laundry. They will leave the collected dirty laundry in the laundry room (or dressing rooms) for the maintenance crew, along with a list of any repairs needed. The maintenance crew will come in and do the laundry and any repairs. They might also do the pressing and steaming of costumes that are not being laundered. This method cuts down on the amount of time the wardrobe crew must stay after the show and how early they are called for pre-show. It also offers opportunities for more students to be part of the crew and offers more intense training in all aspects of wardrobe.

If a student is particularly interested and adept at running wardrobe, I recommend promoting them from wardrobe crew to wardrobe supervisor. At my current institution, I often have a senior student act as the assistant costume designer for a production and then work as the wardrobe supervisor for that same production. Their familiarity with the costumes from being involved in the process from day one is extremely valuable when they transition to the wardrobe supervisor role. It also helps them think about the process from both sides. When we are in fittings, they are also thinking about quick-changes, possible underdressing, quick-rigging needs, and practicality. Conversely, when they are working as the wardrobe supervisor, they know how the costume designer intended for items to be worn and what costumes are to be worn for which scenes. This is often a capstone experience for senior students in the costume design and technology concentration, and it is extraordinarily valuable for their learning and future careers.

I try to encourage students who thrive working on the wardrobe crew to consider summer work in the industry while they are undergraduate students. The curriculum at my current institution requires an advanced internship or advanced production experience, but I try to encourage the students to go for the internship if at all possible. Wardrobe work can provide a steady income for students after graduation, even if it is not their ultimate career goal. I offer training in wardrobe to all of the undergraduate students I can, regardless of their primary concentration or major. Because of the wide variety of professional opportunities available in wardrobe, I encourage students to pursue wardrobe training.

PUTTING IT ALL TOGETHER

How can you teach someone to be good at wardrobe? It is one of those things that it seems some people are naturally good at, and others struggle with. As this chapter has stated, hands-on experience is the best way to learn how to run wardrobe. However, a hands-on teaching approach utilizing best practices can lead students in the right direction and greatly increase their chances of success. If you are a professor and your program could support a wardrobe class (or it could be a portion of the costuming class or another class where it could be appropriate), here is a suggested curriculum outline (see Table 9.1):

Table 9.1 Introduction to Wardrobe Management: Course Outline.

Dates	Topic	Assignments
Week 1	Introduction to Wardrobe Overview of Wardrobe Job Descriptions Theater Hierarchy	Read Introduction: The Importance of Wardrobe Discussion #1: Personal Intro
Week 2	Job Duties Character Traits and Skills Unique Challenges	Read Ch. 1: The Wardrobe Supervisor Discussion #2: Chapter 1 Response Questions
Week 3	Preparing to Work on a Show Communication with the Production Team Analyzing the Script	Read Ch. 2: Pre-Production Quiz #1: Intro and Chapter 1 Discussion #3: Chapter 2 Response Questions
Week 4	Planning and Organization Reading the Piece List	Read Ch. 3: Paperwork Quiz #2: Chapter 2 Discussion #4: Chapter 3 Response Questions
Week 5	Paperwork Samples and Formats Document Design	Assignment: Actor Dressing Lists Discussion #5: What Makes Good Paperwork?
Week 6	Running the Crew Working with Performers	Quiz #3: Chapter 3 Read Chapter 4: Being a Team Leader Discussion #6: Reflection on a Good Leader
Week 7	Creating an Inclusive Backstage Atmosphere Collaborating with Stage Management	Discussion #7: What Makes a Positive Atmosphere? Quiz #4: Chapter 4 Assignment: Check-In Sheets
Week 8	**SPRING BREAK**	
Week 9	Lights Wardrobe Apron: What's In It? In Case of Emergency How to Set Up Backstage Changing Areas	Read Ch. 5: Tools and Safety Assignment: Preset Lists Discussion #8: Safety First
Week 10	Attending a Run-through Dress Rehearsals Quick-Changes Wig and Makeup Changes	Quiz #5: Chapter 5 Read Ch. 6: Tech Week Assignment: Quick-Change Plan and Execution Discussion #9: Let's Talk About TECH

Table 9.1 Introduction to Wardrobe Management: Course Outline. *(Continued)*

Dates	Topic	Assignments
Week 11	Dressing Room Organization In-Class Exercise: Quick-Changes	Quiz #6: Chapter 6 Discussion #10: Problem-Solving
Week 12	Refining Your Routine Consistency of the Integrity of the Design Assigning Tracks Maintaining the Costumes	Read Chapter 7: Performances Discussion #11: How to Give Notes Assignment: Crew Run Sheets
Week 13	In Class Exercise: Pressing and Steaming	Quiz #7: Chapter 7 Assignment: Laundry Charts Discussion #12: Maintenance How-To Video
Week 14	Strike Rental Returns Costume Stock Organization Creating a Record	Read Chapter 8: Next Steps Discussion #13: Let's Take This Show on the Road
Week 15	In Class Work on Wardrobe Plans Q&A	Quiz #8: Chapter 8 Discussion #14: Importance of Wardrobe
Week 16	Finals Week: Present Wardrobe Plans	Discussion #15: Reflection

This is a sample breakdown of assignments and points:

Assignment	Due Date	Points
Discussions (15)	Weekly	150 (10 each)
Quizzes (8)	February 10, February 17, March 3, March 10, Mar 31, April 7, April 21, May 5	200 (25 each)
Actor Dressing Lists	February 24	50
Check-In Sheets	March 10	50
Preset Lists	March 24	50
Quick-Change Plan and Execution	March 31	150
Crew Run Sheets	April 14	50
Laundry Charts	April 21	50
Final: Wardrobe Plan for a Show	May 12	250
	TOTAL	**1,000**

For this curriculum, I recommend using a show that you have paperwork for already and that you know well. Musicals are a great option because they often require multiple quick-changes and tend to have larger casts, so writing tracks for them is a good project. Mixing paperwork creation with hands-on activities will keep the course interesting while helping students gain the knowledge and skills needed to run wardrobe successfully.

CHAPTER 10

Working in Wardrobe

INTERNSHIPS AND APPRENTICESHIPS

If you ask different people who work backstage in live entertainment what their first professional experience was, many of them would probably say an internship or apprenticeship. My first professional wardrobe experience was part of my costuming internship at Surflight Theatre in Beach Haven, NJ, during the summer between my junior and senior years of college. I am still in touch with some of the people I worked with that summer, and it was a formative experience in my career. Internships and apprenticeships are a great way to get your feet wet as a young professional or someone wanting to work in the industry for the first time. As a professor, I encourage all my students to seek internship and apprenticeship opportunities and see tremendous growth in those that heed my advice.

Internships and apprenticeships vary wildly, so there is a lot to consider when you start looking at opportunities. The biggest difference is that some opportunities are seasonal, often for the summer, while others are season long, often running for nine months or more. Depending on your situation, one of these might be more feasible than another. Another consideration is whether the internship or apprenticeship is departmental or more broad. This means that some employers will look for candidates who want to specialize in one area such as wardrobe or costuming, while others look for candidates who are interested in a variety of experiences and interns/apprentices will work some of the time in a variety of departments throughout their internship/apprenticeship. Sometimes you will find that wardrobe is combined with costuming or with hair and makeup or both. If it is combined with costuming, you may spend time working in the costume shop constructing costumes for the show in addition to running wardrobe and if it is combined with hair and makeup, you may spend time styling wigs and assisting with wig maintenance in addition to running wardrobe. Depending on what your skills are and what you are hoping to learn from an internship/apprenticeship, it is important to clarify what the job duties will be for each position you are applying for.

Summer opportunities tend to be offered by theaters operating in vacation destinations that run festivals or other summer-only programming. Sometimes they are located on college campuses and provide housing in the dormitories. They may or may not be affiliated with the college in some way. Summer opportunities can be for Shakespeare Festivals, operas, musical theater productions, new and devised work, and more. The great thing about summer opportunities is that you can pursue them while you are in college between spring and fall semesters, and they are generally shorter contracts, so you can get professional credit without making a long-term commitment. Many summer jobs will offer housing in addition to pay, so it is a great way to get to live in an area you might not otherwise get to experience. Often the locations of summer theaters are beautiful vacation destinations, so the cost of living there in the summer could be pricey if housing is not included. Summer work is very popular among college students, graduate students, and those who work in colleges as faculty and staff, so the competition for positions can be intense. If you are looking at internships and apprenticeships for the first time, I recommend applying for as many opportunities as possible with varying levels of organizations. The experience of interviewing is always beneficial, even if you are not offered a position, and applying to many opportunities increases your chances of securing a job.

Season-long internships/apprenticeships are offered at many regional theaters throughout the United States. These generally run for the length of a company's season, which is often September through May, but can vary depending on programming. Season-long internships are a great way to gain experience on many productions and work with lots of different people. Researching what the company's programming will be for the season you are applying to work there is a smart way to determine if the work they are doing interests you. Regional theaters are often located in larger cities throughout the country, so seeking an opportunity in a city you would be interested in living in or exploring is a great way to narrow your search.

Internships/apprenticeships sometimes provide housing and usually provide compensation in the form of a stipend. Before applying for these opportunities, be sure to research what is provided and what the compensation is and that it is feasible for you and your living situation. These entry-level positions are a great way to gain professional experience and exposure in the industry, but it is imperative that you are able to support yourself with the compensation (and possible housing) provided. If you have student debt, you are sometimes able to defer payments if you are working as an intern/apprentice. Lining up a summer contract followed by a season-long contract with a different company is a great way to plan your first year following college graduation. However, try not to stay at the intern/apprentice level for too long. Some companies will offer you a second-year apprenticeship, sometimes referred to as a journeyman. This can be a great opportunity to get more experience, hone your skills, and be given more responsibility if you are enjoying working for that company. Internships/apprenticeships are meant to be a first step in your career and often offer your first professional credit, but a good intern/apprentice program should prepare you for an entry-level staff position in the field. Some companies may even ask if you would be interested in returning at a staff-level position after successfully completing an internship/apprenticeship.

HOW TO FIND A JOB

Looking for jobs working backstage for live performance can sometimes be confusing. It isn't as easy as going on a career opportunity website and typing in "wardrobe" and having page after page of listings pop up. Actually, it is that easy, but only if you know where to look. There are many great resources for job opportunities in the theatre industry. One of the most longstanding has been **ARTSEARCH**®, which is a service of the Theatre Communications Group (TCG). When I was in college, it was actually a publication that was delivered to most college campuses with a Theatre Department that would get posted on the callboard and we would take turns looking through it for job opportunities and graduate school assistantships (but I digress). **ARTSEARCH**® is now a wonderful online resource that is offered free of charge (it also used to be subscription-based). You do need to create a free account, but the benefit is that you can sign up to receive email alerts for the types of jobs you are specifically interested in, and it will notify you if new jobs meeting your specified criteria are posted. **Offstage Jobs** is another great online resource for finding job opportunities. There are categories you can click on that narrow the job listings by type or city, so it is easy to find what you are looking for. **Playbill** also has a great job board on its' website, and the jobs are not limited to the New York City area, so be sure to check it out.

 The United States Institute for Theatre Technology (USITT) is an industry-leading organization for connecting live entertainment professionals. They have a yearly national conference, which is an amazing experience to attend. Part of the conference includes an expo floor and many companies have booths there that are looking to hire seasonal, temporary, or full-time employees. Attending the United States Institute for Theatre Technology conference and bringing your business card with a link to your website and talking to as many people as possible is a great way to find a job and network with many industry professionals at one time. USITT also has a website with a jobs tab that features a comprehensive listing of job opportunities. They also have a Facebook page that you can follow, which updates frequently with job listings.

Speaking of Facebook, there are many great Facebook groups you can join and follow for job listings. Some are region- or city-specific, some are for specific types of work (such as wardrobe), some are specifically for theatre educators, and additional groups are more broad, listing many opportunities nationwide. The Facebook group that I am a member of that posts lots of backstage jobs is called Quick-Change-Entertainment Job Network-Technical/Production/Administration. You have to request to join and answer some questions and agree to the group rules, but it is a wonderful resource for job listings.

If there is a specific company or theater that you are interested in working for, their website can often be the best place to find job opportunities. If you don't see any opportunities currently listed, it doesn't hurt to check back periodically, as companies will often update at a certain time of year, especially those hiring seasonal positions. LinkedIn can be a great resource to find out if anyone you know has worked at, or knows someone who works for, a company that you are interested in. The live performance industry is all about connections, so if you are able to find someone who is willing to put in a good word for you, it can open the door for an opportunity. Keeping your LinkedIn profile and professional website up to date with information and examples of your work helps potential employers see that you are a great candidate.

UNIONS

First and foremost, I am not a member of a wardrobe or labor union. It is important to understand that there are many different unions and this information is not comprehensive. It is intended to introduce the idea of wardrobe unions and present some information to consider regarding union membership. For further information, you will want to read the information regarding the specific union you are considering joining.

The most well-known labor union in our industry is the International Alliance of Theatrical Stage Employees (IATSE). IATSE is divided into local unions, which include specific departments (such as stage employees). Depending on the region, there may also be a local chapter of the Theatrical Wardrobe Union (TWU), which is a charter of IATSE specifically representing hair, makeup, and wardrobe professionals. IATSE/TWU contracts with venues in a specific area to staff their live events. If a venue is a union house, there will be specific rules about who can and cannot work there and what nonunion staff can and cannot do onsite. If you are confused about anything regarding union regulations and a venue or company you are working for, be sure to clarify these details before reporting for work so that you do not unintentionally violate union regulations.

Unions can be beneficial for workers. Collective bargaining helps get workers better wages, equal compensation, meal break penalties, and education and training. Union work is especially good if you are setting out for a career in wardrobe, because of benefits such as healthcare and pensions/annuities. The call list structure for local unions can vary depending on membership. Some go by seniority while others work on a rotation. If you are interested in local union membership, the IATSE website has contact information for all of their locals. IATSE offers training and education to its members, so it is a great way to hone your skills and learn more about your craft.

NONUNION WORK

Some large, nonunion staging companies also keep a list of local personnel to call for specific productions. The companies I am familiar with are NRG Staging and Rhino Staging because of the time I spent in the Southwest, but there are more companies like this throughout the country. These companies contract with venues to staff specific events and will contract personnel according to the needs of the production, which can be anything from concerts to sports to trade shows and more. If you are located in a city, explore staging companies in the area and find out if they are looking for wardrobe professionals to add to their database.

Regional theaters and opera companies often utilize local professionals for overhire. Overhire refers to positions that are temporary, often for the run of a show. Overhire positions can be paid hourly or at a flat rate per show. If you are working for a flat rate, be sure that the call time and end time are set prior to accepting the rate (so that you can figure out what the hourly amount is). If there are many theaters in your area, getting on the overhire list for all of them is a great way to fill time in between other jobs.

Other options for wardrobe work include cruise ships and theme parks. Often these opportunities will not be listed on the traditional theater job sites I mentioned earlier, and are sometimes only found on the company's own website. If there is a theme park or cruise ship company you would like to work for, start by visiting their website and looking at their employment opportunities. These opportunities can be easier to get without knowing someone than a regional theater, so they can be a great place to start building your network.

TOURING

National and local tours are a great way to get started working in wardrobe. Tours can vary in length from a month or two up to a year or longer. Tours will often employ a wardrobe supervisor and an assistant wardrobe supervisor or two and then fill additional wardrobe needs with local workers who are different at each stop along the way. Touring is a great way to travel while getting paid and having all of your living expenses covered (as the tours pay for lodging while on tour and the transportation to each stop). You can explore cities that you may have never been to and get a feel for where you might want to live after you stop touring. It also gives you the unique experience of building a show at each location and then tearing it down and moving it to the next stop and building it again. Thinking of wardrobe work in this context changes your view of organization and efficiency. Tours may require you to get your union card to work for them, and they may help you do this if they offer you a job. If you are able to work on a tour and not have the expense of rent or a mortgage at home, you can often save a good bit of your salary. Some of my most memorable wardrobe experiences were working as a local for tours that came through Phoenix, AZ, and I have always wished I had worked on a tour when I was younger. Some companies to start with if you are looking for tour opportunities are **NETworks** and **Work Light** productions.

NETWORKING

You have heard me say this already in this book, and you have probably heard it before, the theatre industry is all about who you know. Sometimes, this can be discouraging and have you thinking that you will never get your first job. I'm here to reassure you that it can be just the opposite, and that you should think of every opportunity or encounter as a chance to set you up for your future successes. When I applied for my internship at Surflight Theatre, I didn't know anyone who worked there or had worked there in the past. The faculty at my college did not have experience in costuming or wardrobe work, so it was up to me to figure things out. They were helpful with my resume, cover letter, and portfolio, but beyond that, they had little advice to offer. I applied for many internships that summer, and I was offered two opportunities. This was a pretty good first attempt at professional employment. I attended graduate school straight out of undergrad. There are varying opinions about this, but it worked for me, and I was confident I had more to learn before starting my career full-time. Between my summer at Surflight and starting graduate school at The University of Cincinnati's College Conservatory of Music, pursuing an MFA in Costume Design & Technology, my networking journey began. My costume technology professor, Regina Truhart, knew the Costume Director of The Glimmerglass Festival in Cooperstown, NY, and encouraged me to apply for a staff position as a Stitcher in the Costume Shop. I was lucky enough to be offered the position after interviewing and submitting my portfolio, and I then learned one of the biggest lessons of my career. Because I was going to work at Glimmerglass on Gina's recommendation, I had to be the best of the best. I had to be impressive and do an amazing job because if I didn't, it might jeopardize her reputation and ruin that opportunity for future students. I like to think that I upheld my end of this bargain, as I was offered a position as a First Hand at Glimmerglass the following summer, which is a promotion. I was then unable to do summer work for many years because I held year-round positions at regional theaters across the country, but since becoming an Assistant Professor at Albright College, I have been able to return to the Glimmerglass Festival in the summers. I spent last summer there as a Draper and I am looking forward to spending the upcoming summer as the Wardrobe Manager. One of the regional theater jobs I had was offered to me because of connections at Glimmerglass and graduate school. The point of this narrative is that you never know what connection you have that could help open a door for your future. As you continue in your career, you may become the connection that opens the door for someone behind you. It is important to remember to always try your best and work well with others, especially if you have been given an opportunity on the recommendation of someone else. It is important that their reputation remain in good standing and that you begin to build your own positive reputation.

We can get overwhelmed by social media these days, but it is a great way to stay in touch with people whom you meet at various jobs. You never know where somebody is going to end up, so having a way to stay in touch with your connections and allowing them to stay in touch with you strengthens your network and expands your resources. Also, your friends might be the first to post about a new job opportunity, even before it is made public. Following your connections on social media platforms alerts you to opportunities so you can be the first applicant to your dream job.

WARDROBE AS A CAREER

Even though many people have no idea what you mean when you say that you work in wardrobe, I'm here to tell you that you can have a successful career in this field if you want to. If you enjoy the fast-paced nature of working backstage and have the skills and personality to run wardrobe successfully, there are many rewarding employment opportunities awaiting you. If you take a look in the program for the next show you go to, notice how many names are listed as wardrobe crew or dressers. Compare this to some of the other departments, and you may be surprised at how many opportunities there are for wardrobe professionals. Many regional theaters employ a full-time wardrobe supervisor or two and some colleges and universities have added this position to their full-time professional staff. In addition to theatre and opera, there are opportunities for cruise ships, theme parks, concerts, sporting events, expos, trade shows, film, television, fashion, and more. I encourage you to explore as many different opportunities as you can and find what you love so that you can have a long and rewarding career.

Resources

Here is a listing of my favorite sources for wardrobe and quick-rigging supplies. This list is not comprehensive, and if you find a great source for wardrobe supplies, please let me know so I can add their information to this list.

The Costume Source

https://thecostumesource.com/

252 West 38th Street, Room #1005, New York, NY 10018

Manhattan Wardrobe Supply

https://www.wardrobesupplies.com/

245 W 29th St, 8th Floor, New York, NY 10001

Ninja

https://ninjasgo.com/

Las Vegas, NV

Wawak

https://www.wawak.com/

1059 Powers Road, Conklin, NY 13748

HAIR STYLING PRODUCT RECOMMENDATIONS

If you are purchasing hair products and supplies to use for wig maintenance and for performers who are styling their own hair for the show, it can be overwhelming to know what to buy. I asked Kelly Yurko what products she recommends, and she sent me the following list.

PLEASE NOTE, THESE ARE **SOME** SUGGESTIONS.

THIS IS IN NO WAY A COMPLETE LIST OF HAIR PRODUCTS THAT CAN BE USED.

Combs and Brushes	Hair Gel-Various Types	Tools and Supplies
Rat Tail Comb	Got2B Glued®, all types	Spray Bottle for Water
Five Prong Comb	Eco Style Gels®, all types	Spray Bottle for Water and Setting Lotion
Wire Hairbrush	SheaMoisture® Defining Styling Gel	Spray Bottle for Water and Gel

Bristle Hairbrush	Tresemme® Hair Gel	End Papers for roller setting
Edge Brush	Aussie® Sculpting Gel	Hair Setting Lotion
Hair Wire Pick	LA Looks® Sport Gel	Corsage/Pearl Pins-2" or larger
Pomades and Waxes	Aunt Jackie's® Flaxseed Don't Shrink Curling Gel	Bias Tape for Blocking Wigs
Suavecita® Pomade for Women	Moco de Gorila® Punk Styling Gel	Sewing Pins 1.5" or shorter
Suavecito® Pomade for Men	Mielle Organics® Strengthening Edge Gel	**Hair Rollers: Various Sizes, Shapes and Types**
Carol's Daughter® Mimosa Hair Honey Shine Pomade	Let's Jam® Protein and Shine Gel	Flexible Rods Various Sizes and Types
Groom & Clean®	ILIOS African Formulas® SuperGrow Hair Gel	Wire Mesh Rollers Various Sizes
Brylcreem®	Braid Gel	Plastic Rollers
GATSBY® Moving Rubber Air Rise Hair Wax	KeraCare GelEssence® Super Hold Gel	Hot Rollers
Murray's® Superior Hair Dressing Pomade	Edge Gel, various types	Curling Irons-Various Sizes and Types
Murray's® Edgewax		[a] Other objects for hair setting
Hair Sprays	Heat Protectant Sprays	**Shine Sprays**
AquaNet®	CHI® 44 Iron Guard	CHI® Shine Infusion Hair Shine
Tresemme®	Straight™ Silk Spray	Color WOW® Dream Coat Supernatural Spray
Got2b® Glued	Hair Food Coconut and Argan Oil	African Pride® Olive Miracle Magical Growth Sheen Spray
CHI®	Mielle® Mongongo	Originals® Africa's Best Tea-Tree
Paul Mitchell®	[b]	Cantu® Coconut Oil Shine and Hold Mist with Shea Butter for Natural Hair

[a] Other objects for hair setting can include
  Drinking straws
  Chopsticks
  Strips of fabric
  Bobby pins

[b] These are suggestions. This is in no way a complete list of hair products that can be used. These products work well for me and/or I like the smell. If I do not like the way a product smells, I tend not to use it.

USEFUL WEBSITES

ARTSEARCH

https://tcg.org/ (click on ARTSEARCH at the top)

IATSE

https://iatse.net/join/

Offstage Jobs

https://staging.offstagejobs.com/jobs.php

Playbill (Jobs)

https://playbill.com/jobs

USITT

https://www.usitt.org/

Author Biography

It was inevitable that I would end up working in theatre. At least that's what my dad said when we were discussing my biography for this book. And he is right. My parents started taking me to plays when I was 4 years old, and we saw the National Tour of *Cats* in Philadelphia. I was mesmerized and inspired. I started acting lessons at 5 and dance classes at 6. I did competition team dance until age 18 and then became a dance minor as I started college. I performed in all of the plays and musicals during high school and my mom and I would help make all of the costumes. My mom taught me to sew at age 5. My dad has an M.A. in Theatre from Villanova University and played the lead in many of his high school productions. My mom was on the stage crew in college. My dad attended the Stratford Festival in Canada for over 40 seasons and my mom and I joined him for many of them. I started my college career as a musical theatre major and dance minor at Wilkes University in Pennsylvania. As part of our work in the major, we had to work in the shops to help build the shows. I was assigned to the costume shop for the first show because I had sewing experience. And it was there that I fell in love. I loved everything about it. Cutting, sewing, alterations, costume design, fittings, and crafts. I found my passion and my place in the theatre, and I have never looked back. I must thank Adam Hill and Joe Dawson for this, their guidance pushed me into the career of my dreams.

    I transferred for my junior and senior years to Albright College in Reading, PA. They had a co-major in Fashion & Theatre that would allow me to graduate on time and take courses in patternmaking, draping, CAD, fashion design, costume design, and rendering. I got to co-design the costumes for a show my first semester at Albright and had a solo costume design my senior year. I worked in the costume shop building costumes and continued appearing onstage. Julia Matthews was one of my mentors at Albright (and now a dear colleague) and she encouraged me to pursue a costuming internship for the summer. I landed a costuming internship at Surflight Theatre in Beach Haven, NJ, and it was there that I ran Wardrobe as I now know it for the first time. We did big musicals with a lot of cast members, many costume changes, and lots of logistics. The other interns and I figured it out the best we could, and the performers were gracious, helpful, and patient. I knew that this was what I wanted to do, and I set out to do it.

    I pursued my M.F.A. in Costume Design & Technology at the University of Cincinnati's College Conservatory of Music. I spent the summers in between the years at The Glimmerglass Festival, first as a stitcher and then as a first hand. I got a job after graduating at The Shakespeare Theatre in Washington, DC, as a stitcher. I relocated to be the Assistant Costume Shop Manager at The Phoenix Theatre Company in Arizona and was eventually promoted to Costume Shop Manager. While in Phoenix, I was blessed to work as a wardrobe local on many concerts and National Tours. After 6 years there, I decided to pursue a career in higher education.

I worked as the Costume Shop Manager and an Adjunct Professor at the University of Texas-Rio Grande Valley. Then I was a Visiting Assistant Professor and the Costume Studio Manager at the University of Louisiana at Lafayette. From there, I became the Costume Shop Manager and an Adjunct Professor at Kean University's Theatre Conservatory and Premiere Stages Theatre Company. At this point, my dream job entered the picture. Albright College (my alma mater) was hiring an Assistant Professor of Theatre to run the costume studio for the Theatre Department and teach costuming and related courses. I'm happy to say that I got it and returned to the place that gave me so much as an undergraduate. Jeff Lentz and Julia Matthews were my mentors when I was a student, and I am so lucky to get to work with them as my colleagues on this amazing adventure along with Jen Rock and Matt Fotis. I have dedicated student workers and production experience students in the costume studio and a wonderful collaboration with the Fashion Department to offer a Costume Design track through the Theatre Department. Because my contract offers summer flexibility, I have returned to the Glimmerglass Festival. For the 2023 season, I worked as a Draper on *Candide*. For the 2024 season, I will be working as the Wardrobe Manager, overseeing assistant managers, wardrobe staff, and wardrobe apprentices.

Glossary

Actor Piece List: (AKA dressing lists) The list of costume pieces that an actor wears for a production, which indicates which pieces they wear when, including all accessories

Bite Light: A small flashlight with a flexible plastic or leather case that you put in your mouth and operate with your teeth. It can be worn on a lanyard around your neck for hands-free operation

Check-In Sheets: A checklist of all the individual costume pieces and accessories used for a show that is divided by performer and/or preset location and has columns for each performance date

Closure: A button, snap, zipper, fabric tie, or other fastener that closes a garment

Crew Run Sheets: The list of tasks that a wardrobe crew member performs from start to finish for a single performance, including all pre-show responsibilities, presets, quick-changes, tracking of costumes, post-show duties, and more

Crossover: An area out of the view of the audience upstage that allows crew and performers to travel from one side of the stage to the other without being seen

Cue to Cue: A rehearsal that jumps from one cue to the next, skipping over the scenes or songs in between, thus only rehearsing each cue or transition

Darning: Done by hand or machine, a method of filling in a hole in a piece of clothing with thread and reinforcing it

Deck: The onstage area and the backstage area, where the flooring changes

Ditty Bags: Hanging accessory bags labeled with the names of performers that organize all accessories such as shoes, jewelry, hosiery, neckties, scarves, headwear, and more

Gaff(er's) Tape: A 2" wide tape made of fabric that can be used for quick repairs backstage that most commonly comes in white and black

Gondolas: Large, rolling cases with a hanging bar for costumes that have two sides that swing open and can be latched together when closed for easy transportation

"Hit by a Bus" Theory: The author's overarching philosophy that information should be shared freely, and it is important to keep others in the loop because you never know when the unexpected may happen

House: The area of the theater where the audience sits

Masking: Curtains or other materials used to give a space privacy or hide it from view

Men's Grooming Tape: Double-sided, clear tape that comes in a variety of widths for temporarily attaching fake facial hair to one's face

Millinery: The process of constructing or reworking hats and headwear

Preset List: List of the costume pieces needed for presets (*see presets*)

Presets: Costume pieces that need to be placed in specific locations before a show for quick-changes that will take place during the show

Pressing: (AKA ironing) Using an iron and ironing board or table to remove wrinkles from a garment, often by using the steam setting

Quick-Change: When a performer changes from one costume to another during a performance and their allotted time is less than five minutes or possibly longer but the pieces involved are numerous or complicated

Quick-Change Booth: (QCB) An area backstage designated for costume quick-changes that is given some form of privacy screening, such as pipe-and-drape curtains or temporary walls

Quick-Rigging: Changing the existing closure of a garment to make it quicker to put on or take off; can include changing buttons to snaps or Velcro™ or hooks and eyes to a zipper

Remount: When a production that was produced in a past season is done again at the same venue

Run-Through: A rehearsal where the actors perform the show in order without stopping to the best of their ability without technical elements, usually in a rehearsal facility

Skins: Clothing items that serve as a base layer and make direct contact with the performer's skin, such as dance belts, hosiery, undershirts, bras, and dance trunks

Stage Management: The department responsible for running live performances, including calling all technical cues and actor entrances and exits, ensuring all personnel are present at specified call times, creating reports from rehearsals and productions, recording blocking in rehearsals, taking meeting minutes, communicating schedules, and more

Steaming: Using a steamer, which is a large tank of heated water attached to a plastic or metal hose with an end that has holes on it to release the steam gradually, to remove the wrinkles from clothing

Strike: The process at the end of the run of a show when all the departments restore the venue to its original condition and the wardrobe department cleans all the costumes and accessories and returns or restocks them

Tech: (AKA technical rehearsals) The rehearsals leading up to the opening of a production where all the technical elements (lights, costumes, scenery, props, sound, hair and makeup, etc.) are incorporated into the production

Track: The tasks that a wardrobe crew member performs from start to finish for a single performance, including all pre-show responsibilities, presets, quick-changes, tracking of costumes, post-show duties, and more

Tracking: Moving a costume piece from one location to another either after a costume change or to prepare for one

Wardrobe: The department responsible for the dressing, care, and cleaning of costumes for live performance

Wardrobe Apron: Waist apron work by wardrobe personnel that contains items they could need while working backstage, such as safety pins, seam ripper, lint roller, and more

Wardrobe Crew: The staff of people working backstage of a live production who are responsible for the dressing, care, preparation, and cleaning of the costumes

Wardrobe Supervisor: The manager of the wardrobe department and wardrobe crew who is responsible for creating or delegating the creation of wardrobe paperwork, managing the wardrobe staff, solving problems, and ensuring things run smoothly for the wardrobe department

Bibliography

Cunningham, Rebecca and Brooklyn College. *The Magic Garment: Principles of Costume Design*. Longman 1989.

Ingham, Rosemary and Covey, Liz. *The Costume Technician's Handbook*. Third ed. Heinemann, 2003.

Kincman, L. *The Stage Manager's Toolkit*. Focal Press, 2013.

Index

Note: Locators in *italics* represent figures in the text.

abbreviations, usage of 36
accessory organizers *15*
accessory storage 95, *96*, 117
actor piece lists 30, 83
Actor's Equity Association rules 39, 51, 80, 102, 107
adhesive hooks 74
alcohol wipe 92, 94
anti-fatigue mats 61
apprenticeships 133–135
apron *20*, 23, 33, 64, 65–67, 70, 86, 94, 98
artificial facial hair 93, 110
ASM *see* assistant stage manager
assistant stage manager (ASM) 56, 80, 81, 101
asthma attack 59–60
As You Like It 12, *31*, *32*, 37, *38*, 84

back injury 59
backstage atmosphere 49, 51, 53–54
backstage changing areas 37, 45, 71; baskets 73–74, *73*; chairs 72–73; gondolas 76–77, *76*, *77*; hooks 74–75; quick-change booths 75–76
backstage environment 50, 53, 54
backstage personnel 71
bacteria, killing 104, 106
baskets, laundry 7, 12, 13, 15, 37, 53, 73–74, *73*, 99, 102
bathrooms, utilization of 51, 82
bite lights 61, *62*, *63*
black clothing 65, 68, 69, 81
bleach 104
blocking a wig 109
bow tie with Velcro™ 18, *19*
box-by-box inventory 118
braids 26, *27*
button-down shirt 18, 20; quick-rigged with necktie 20, *21*; quick-rigged with snaps 21, *22*; quick-rigged with Velcro™ *19*
buttons 18, 20–21, 87

canvas head blocks 109
career, wardrobe as 3, 139–140
cell phone/technology usage in backstage areas 82
chairs 72–73
character traits and skills of wardrobe supervisor 6–7
Check-In sheets 31–33, 37, 84

check-out procedure 31
choreography 26, 55, 87, 88, 90
chorus 25, 51
cleaning fluid 104
clip hangers 95–96
clip lights 53, 61, 64
closure 24, 56, 89, 90
communication 45, 46, 54, 55; with production team 11–13
conversations 53, 54
costume changes 1, 13, 15, 82, 83, 91, 93, 126
costume design 2, 53, 100, 101, 108, 123, 129
costume designer 2, 6, 11, 12, 18, 24, 30, 46, 52, 55, 90, 101, 107, 123, 129
costume load-in 84–86
costume parade 80
costume preset *38*, *89*
costumes 6; load-in process of 84–85; maintaining 101–108; malfunctioning costume piece, dealing with 70; restocking 119; worn for entire show 103; worn for single scene 103; *see also* performances and costume maintenance
Costume Shop Manager 11, 108, 146
costume shop staff 13, 30, 55, 117, 119, 122, 123
Costume Shop Supervisor 30
costumes organized in a dressing room at Albright College *8*
costume stock organization 118–122
costume storage at The Phoenix Theatre Company *120*
craft skills 6, 108
crew members, wardrobe 6, 14, *16*, 17, 33, 37, 39, 47, 53, 56, 68, 80–81, 83, 89, 93, 100, 122, 126
crew run sheets 33–37
crew watch 55, 82
crossover 72, 74, 83
cue-to-cue rehearsals 56, 79

daily wig maintenance 108–111
dance shows 82
darning 108
deck 49, 57, 81
delegation 30, 46, 47
designer run 11, 14, 55, 82, 84
disrespect 48, 52
ditty bags 7, 95
double-sided grooming tape 92, 93

dresser *see* wardrobe crew member
dressing notes 46
dressing rooms 7–8, *8*, 15, 30, 33, 37, *38*, 51, 54, 60, 81–82, 84, 85; costumes hung in *96*; organization of 95–96
dress rehearsals 79, 80, 86–87, 88, 102; during tech week 97; process 52, 56, 58, 87, 107, 126
dry cleaning 43, 117, 122
dryer 43, 104, 115
dry tech 79

elastic 21–22, 61; inside of a shirt cuff quick-rigged with *23*; shirt cuff quick-rigged with *23*
elastic cufflinks 22, *23*
emergency items 71
emergency situation 57, 70–71
entrance/exit chart 11, *12*, 14
entrances and exits: locations of 83; recording 82
Epsom salts 60
equity rules 102
essential oils 105
exercise routine 60
exit time, recording 82

Facebook 136
facial hair 93–94, 110, 111
First Aid/CPR (cardiopulmonary resuscitation) training 71
fishnet stockings 108
flashlights 61, 63
flexibility and mobility 60
football pants quick-rigged with ribbon and snap closure 25, *26*
French cuffs 22
full-length mirrors 77–78

Gaffer's tape 70, 66, 68, 147
The Glimmerglass Festival 15
gondolas 7, 76–77, *76*, *77*, *97*
gravity and drying sweat 110
grooming tape, double-sided 92, *93*
grosgrain ribbon 25

hair and hats, quick rigging with 26
hair and wig styling techniques 7, 110
hairnets 110
hairpins designed for quick-changes *93*
hairstyle 69
hands-on teaching approach 129
hand-washing tasks 43
handwritten notes 29
hanger-based organizers 7
hangers 81, 95–96, *96*
hanging organizers 7, 77, 85, 95, *97*
harness 24
hats 24, 69, 121; stitching hair into 26
headlamps 61, 62, 69
heat-shrink tipping 22
hero track 29

hooks 74–75, *106*
house 83, 127
hydration 61, 98

IATSE *see* International Alliance of Theatrical Stage Employees
importance of wardrobe 1–3
"in case I get hit by a bus" strategy 29
inclusive backstage atmosphere, creating 50–54
information sharing 30
integrity of design, consistency of 100–101
International Alliance of Theatrical Stage Employees (IATSE) 136–137
internships and apprenticeships 133–135

jewelry 69, 108; creation and repair 7; quick rigging 24
job, finding 135–136
job duties of wardrobe supervisor 5–6
jumpsuits 65, 68

labeling the performers' individual stations 85
laundry 102, 115
laundry baskets 7, 13, 37, 73, 99, 102
laundry charts 39–44
laundry schedule 39, *40–42*, 102–103
leadership 46
leggings 68
light backstage 53
light-blocking curtains 119
lights 61–65
lingerie bags *see* zippered laundry bags
LinkedIn 136
load-in process of costumes 84–85
locations of entrances and exits 14, 83
Lysol spray 106

machine and hand darning 108
The Magic Garment (Rebecca Cunningham) 5
magnetic jewelry clasps *24*
magnets 22–24
magnet tape *17*, 23, *24*
maintenance crew 128
makeup changes 90–95
malfunctioning costume piece, dealing with 70
Mary Poppins 65
masking 75
medical emergency 71
mesh bags 102, 104
mesh laundry bags 7, *105*
mesh-style hairnet 110
mic belts 102
microphones, wireless 13, 61, 91
millinery 6
miniature flashlights 63
mirrors, full-length 77–78
multi-pocket hanging organizers 95
muscle therapy 60

musicals 24, 25, 82, 132
muslin bags 102
mustache, artificial *94*
mutual respect 50, 52

nap 98
neck lights 61, 62–63, *64*
necktie 87; button-down shirt quick-rigged with 20, *21*
networking 138–139
nonunion work 137

odors, reducing 104, 106
organization 6, 7–9
overcoat with shirt cuffs attached to the bottom of the sleeves *25*
overheating backstage 68
overhire 137
OxiClean 103, 104

panic 70
pants 25–26, 68, 119; quick-rigged with ribbon and snap closure 25, *26*
paperwork 7, 11, 12, 14, 15, 16, *16*, 29, 117–118; actor piece lists 30; Check-In sheets 31–33; crew run sheets 33–37; laundry charts 39–44; power of 29–30; preset lists 37–38; updating 99–100
performances and costume maintenance 99; daily wig maintenance 108–111; integrity of design, consistency of 100–101; maintaining the costumes 101–108; refining the routine 99–100
performer names, printed sheets with 85
performers, working with 47–50
personality backstage 53
personal jewelry 69
personal lights 61, 65
personal style 67
personnel, wardrobe *see* wardrobe personnel
The Phoenix Theatre Company 11, 30, 33, 39, 55, 102, 115, 146
Piece Lists 30, 31
pigtail braids 26, *27*
pipe-and-drape curtains *75*
planning and organization of pre-production 14–16
plastic hangers 81
pre-production 11; communication with production team 11–13; planning and organization 14–16; quick-rigging tools, tips, and techniques 16–27; script, analyzing 13–14
preset lists 37–38
presets 8, 37, 47, 70, 89, 126
presetting items 89
pressing (ironing) 107
problem-solving 97–98
production managers 11, 71, 117
production stage manager 57, 101, 123
production team, communication with 11–13

QCB *see* quick-change booths
quick-change 13, 56, 83, 87–90
quick-change baskets 73–74, *73*
quick-change booths (QCB) 75–76
quick-change hairpins 92
quick-change rehearsals 80, 88, *93*
quick-change setup backstage *92*
quick-rigging tools and techniques 16–27

rack tags 95
rare-earth magnets 22
record, creating 122–123
recording entrances and exits 82
Red Cross 71
regional theaters 7, 134, 137, 139
remount 17, 44, 122
rental returns 117–118
repairs 108
restocking costumes 119
rolling racks 7
running lights 53
run sheets 33
run-through, attending 82–84

safety and parameters of the job 59–61
safety pins 85
SARD 103
scarf 13–14, 53
season-long internships/apprenticeships 134
self-care 60, 98
sewing skills 6, 27
sew-in magnets, individual *24*
Shakespeare Festivals 134
shirt cuffs 25; attached to the bottom of the sleeves, overcoat with *25*; quick-rigged with elastic *23*
shoelaces 21–22
shoe paint 108
shoe repair 108
shoes 53, 68, 95, 106, *121*
shorts 68
Shout Color Catcher 104
single scene, costumes worn for 103
Sitzprobe 80
sizing 119
skills of wardrobe supervisor 6–7
skin parts, dealing with 102
skins 39
sleep 61, 98
sleeves *25*, 30, 68, 89
small bins 7
snaps *17*, 20, 87; button-down garment with snaps, quick rigging 21; button-down shirt quick-rigged with 21, *22*
snap tape *17*, 20
socks 68, 102
sound engineer 13
sound professionals 24
spirit gum 93–94
stage management, collaborating with 54–58

stage management team 11, 46, 51, 52, 54–55, 57–58, 71
stage manager 11, 39, 51, 53, 55, 57, 123
stain removers and their uses 104
steaming 107
stopwatch 82
store-bought items 43
stove irons 111, *111*
straw bonnet with yarn pigtail braids sewn in *27*
strike 113
strike plan 114–117, *116*
strip lights 64
summer opportunities 134
super glue 70
Surflight Theatre 138

TCG *see* Theatre Communications Group
teaching wardrobe 125; practical experience 127–129; putting it all together 129–132; teaching philosophy 125–127
team leader, being 45; inclusive backstage atmosphere, creating 50–54; performers, working with 47–50; running the crew 45–47; stage management, collaborating with 54–58
tech 79–80
tech rehearsal process 56, 79
tech week 79; costume load-in 84–86; dressing room organization 95–96; dress rehearsals 86–87; hours and expectations 80–82; problem-solving 97–98; quick-changes 87–90; run-through, attending 82–84; wig and makeup changes 90–95
temporary fix 70
Theatre Communications Group (TCG) 135
Theatrical Wardrobe Union (TWU) 136
thermal stoves 110, *111*
tools and safety 59; backstage changing areas, setting up 71–77; emergency situation 70–71; lights 61–65; safety and parameters of the job 59–61; wardrobe apron 65–67; what (and what not) to wear 67–69
touring 138
track 9
tracking 83, 118, 122
training in wardrobe 2
trap doors 83
trial-by-fire 2
TWU *see* Theatrical Wardrobe Union

uncomfortable backstage 54
underdressing 15, 90, 129
undershirts 102, 103
unions 136–137
unique challenges of wardrobe supervisor 9
United States Institute for Theatre Technology (USITT) 135
universities 7
USITT *see* United States Institute for Theatre Technology

Velcro™ *17*, 18, 24, 87, 102; bow tie with *19*; button-down shirt quick-rigged with *19*
vigorous dance number 103
vodka 104–105

waistband 89
wall-mounted hooks 7
wardrobe apron *see* apron
wardrobe crew member 6, 14, *16*, 17, 33, 37, 39, 47, 53, 56, 68, 80–81, 83, 89, 93, 100, 122, 126
wardrobe management 125, 130–131
Wardrobe Manager 15
wardrobe personnel 5, 36, 49, 50
wardrobe spray 104–105, 122, 128
wardrobe team 1–2, 6, 11, 33, 43, 47, 49, 57, 70, 79, 81, 82, 84, 86, 102, 107, 108
washing costume pieces 39, 103
washing machine 110
wet bias tape 109
wig and makeup changes 90–95
Wig and Makeup Designer 11
wig designer 24, 92
wig maintenance, daily 108–111
wigs and facial hair, maintaining 111
wig styling techniques 7
wig with a roller set *109*
wig with curls *110*
wire hangers 81
wireless microphones 13, 61
wooden hangers 96
working in wardrobe 133; career, wardrobe as 139–140; internships and apprenticeships 133–135; job, finding 135–136; networking 138–139; nonunion work 137; touring 138; unions 136–137

yarn pigtail braids, straw bonnet with *27*
yoga 60

zigzag machine stitch 26
zippered laundry bags 7, 102
zippers 17

For Product Safety Concerns and Information please contact our EU representative GPSR@taylorandfrancis.com
Taylor & Francis Verlag GmbH, Kaufingerstraße 24, 80331 München, Germany

www.ingramcontent.com/pod-product-compliance
Lightning Source LLC
Chambersburg PA
CBHW080411300426

44113CB00015B/2482